Out of the Shadows

STEVE DIXON

Other books in the Rumours of the King trilogy, coming soon:

What the Sword Said
The Empty Dragon

Copyright © Steve Dixon 2003
First published 2003
Reprinted 2003, 2004
ISBN 1 85999 671 X

Scripture Union, 207–209 Queensway, Bletchley, Milton Keynes,
MK2 2EB, England.
Email: info@scriptureunion.org.uk
Website: www.scriptureunion.org.uk

Scripture Union Australia
Locked Bag 2, Central Coast Business Centre, NSW 2252
Website: www.su.org.au

Scripture Union USA
P.O. Box 987, Valley Forge, PA 19482
Website: www.scriptureunion.org

The right of Steve Dixon to be identified as author of this work has been
asserted by him in accordance with the Copyright, Designs and Patents Act
1988.

British Library Cataloguing-in-Publication Data.

A catalogue record of this book is available from the British Library.

Printed and bound in Great Britain by Creative Print and Design (Wales)
Ebbw Vale.

Cover: Hurlock Design

↳ Scripture Union is an international Christian charity working with
churches in more than 130 countries, providing resources to bring the good
news about Jesus Christ to children, young people and families and to
encourage them to develop spiritually through the Bible and prayer.

As well as our network of volunteers, staff and associates who run holidays,
church-based events and school Christian groups, we produce a wide range
of publications and support those who use our resources through training
programmes.

FOR MY MUM AND DAD
DOREEN AND BILLY DIXON
to celebrate the storyland of my childhood

CHAPTER ONE

'**N**o! And when I say no, I mean no!'

Ruel's father upended the wooden bowl he was eating from, and tipped the last bit of vegetable stew into his mouth in a way that meant he had said all there was to say. There was a pause – just long enough for his father to start thinking he might have won – then Ruel spoke again.

'But she'll be expecting me,' he said, quietly.

His father, Maaz, lowered the rim of the bowl a fraction and stared at his son. The boy was only twelve but he held onto his father's eyes and did not look away.

Although they seemed rock steady on the outside, both of them had thumping hearts and blood drumming in their ears. The womenfolk – Ruel's mother and sister – held their breath. Little Ezer turned away into the darkest corner of their cramped cottage. He meant to pretend not to notice what was going on and play swords with a stick from the fire kindling. Then he changed his mind. He knew from painful experience that if he made a noise at a time like this he was likely to catch what was meant for Ruel.

There was a thud and Ezer jerked round. He was just in time to see his father's food bowl bounce off the hard earth floor and roll away into the shadows. Ruel jumped a fraction, but stayed where he was, sitting rigid on a length of log by the gently crackling fire. He didn't take his eyes off his father. He tried not to blink, and the smoke that always filled their single room made his eyes burn. On the other side of the flames, his father rose – seeming huge in the tiny space. This was the crisis point and they all knew it. How many times over the years Maaz had chased his son round that fire

5

like some kind of game. Often it had ended in laughter. But not this past year. Something was changing. They lived deep in the forest amongst the creatures of the wild, and they all knew what it meant when males locked horns.

All of a sudden Maaz gave a roar. He took a stride and kicked out – but he had kicked at the wooden bowl where it had come to rest. It crashed into the mud wall, taking a chunk out, and came ricocheting back. Ezer ducked as it flew over his head.

'You talk to him!' Maaz shouted at his wife and kicked again.

This time it was the door. It flew open, and before it had time to swing back shut again the big man had ducked through the frame and was out into the fading light of the evening.

There was a moment's silence whilst everyone tried to take in what had happened, then Ezer piped up from the shadows.

'That nearly hit me! It's always me that gets it!'

He lobbed the bowl at Ruel with a pretend growl, and everyone laughed.

'Give it to me,' said his mother, Naama. 'It needs cleaning.'

'Come and get it!' said Ruel, waving it over his head like a prize.

'If you're keeping it – you can wash it,' his sister, Safir, told him.

'And everyone else's,' said Naama.

He admitted defeat and tossed it gently back to his mother.

Ruel felt relieved. They all did. Actually, he felt a bit like crying. Safir came to squat down beside him and put her arm round his shoulder. She confused him these days, just like he confused himself. She'd always been his playmate, but now, at sixteen, she sometimes felt more like another mother. His eyes were pricking and he wiped them on his rough woollen sleeve.

'Stupid smoke,' he said. 'I don't think any of it goes out of that at all.' He pointed to the hole in the roof that was standard in the cottages of Hazar.

'If you want a proper chimney, that means living in a town – like Kiriath,' his sister reminded him.

'And that means money,' Naama went on, 'which we haven't got.'

'And leaving here,' said Ezer, 'and all our friends.'

Ezer had got them back to what had started the argument with Maaz, and they all went quiet. Naama gathered the eating things into the basket ready to take down to the river for washing. Maaz had told her to talk to Ruel and she knew she'd have to. She wasn't furious about the situation like Maaz, but she *did* agree with him – Ruel shouldn't go. She must speak.

But it was Ruel himself who kicked the discussion off again.

'What harm can it do?' he asked. He was staring into the fire and sounded as if he was talking to himself. 'She's just an old woman.'

'Then why are you bothered about going to see her?' Ezer put in.

'She's *not* just an old woman,' Naama reminded Ruel, 'she's Zilla.'

'She's a witch,' Ezer muttered.

'She's just strange,' Naama said. 'She upsets people.'

Ezer asked Ruel what he *did* when he went to see Zilla, and his brother told him they just talked, mostly. Ezer thought that sounded boring.

'It's not,' Ruel explained, 'that's the point. She tells the most amazing stories.'

'That's what your father's worried about,' Naama butted in. 'He's worried she'll give you ideas.'

'Is it bad to have ideas?' Safir asked, quietly.

'It depends what they are,' her mother replied.

'Anyway – why all the fuss all of a sudden?' Ruel asked. 'I've been going to see her for years – ever since the time she pulled me out of the river.'

'I know,' said Naama. 'We owe your life to Zilla – we know that, but – times change, you're getting older, you'll be a man soon…'

Ezer burst out laughing and Ruel would have punched him if Safir hadn't got in between them.

'Your father doesn't want her to give you the wrong ideas – that's all,' Naama went on.

'What kind of ideas are those?' Ruel asked.

'You know very well. You've got to face it, Ruel, she's an outcast – she's lucky she hasn't been driven right away into the forest. And anyone who spends time with an outcast gets to be – well – an outcast themselves. Your father's worried. He's been worried for a long time. He blames himself for not having done something about it before. I blame myself. We've not been good parents to you, Ruel—'

'Because you've let me talk to an old woman that nobody else will talk to? That's stupid!'

His mother just stared at him. She didn't shout and throw things like his father, but he could see she was upset.

'We just want what's best for you,' Naama said, after a while.

'How do you know what's best for me?' Ruel muttered.

'We don't want you to turn out like her.'

Ruel looked his mother straight in the face.

'I can't think of any better way to turn out,' he said.

His face was set hard and Naama thought how very like

Maaz he looked. She knew that as far as Ruel was concerned, *he* had now said all there was to say.

The boy turned away and went to sit in the corner with his little brother. He picked up a stick and started fencing with Ezer, but neither of them put much enthusiasm into it. After a while Safir started things off again. 'Why is Zilla expecting you tonight?' she said.

Ruel answered without turning. 'It's a special day – an anniversary.'

'What anniversary?' Safir asked him.

'It's the day that Hanan was taken away,' Naama said, quietly.

Ruel looked at her, surprised.

'Zilla isn't the only one who remembers,' she said.

'Who's Hanan?' Ezer asked.

Ruel looked as if he was going to say something, but his mother cut in quickly.

'No one,' she said. 'No one important. It was a long time ago. That's another thing that worries your father—' speaking to Ruel now '—he doesn't want you carrying this on.' She gave a glance at Ezer. 'The man *should* be forgotten.'

Another silence. Ruel and Ezer tried drawing something on the mud floor with their sticks, but it was hopeless – there were no windows, and the only light came from the fire – they couldn't see a thing. Naama put some wood on the fire, but it didn't help much. Safir hooked the strap of the basket on her shoulder and lifted it as if she was going to the river to wash the food things, but then she didn't move.

'Mum,' Safir said, putting down the basket, 'if you don't want Ruel to visit Zilla any more – he ought to go and *tell* her, shouldn't he? It's not fair otherwise – if he doesn't turn up now and then doesn't ever go near her again, she might think he doesn't like her any more. If *you're* stopping him, he ought to tell her it's your fault he's not coming any more – then it's all straight and honest and she knows what's what. At the very least, he ought to say goodbye.'

She turned to Ruel. 'If you go and see her now, will you make it the last time, and say goodbye?' she asked.

He nodded.

'Mum?' she asked, 'what do you think?'

Naama swept the ash and the mess from their meal out of the door before she replied. She was proud of her daughter. Actually, she was proud of Ruel. She wasn't very proud of Maaz and herself, or anyone else in the village.

'I suppose you're right,' she said.

Safir heaved the basket on her shoulder again and made for the door.

'I'll go and see what Dad thinks,' she said. 'I know where he'll be.'

<hr>

When Safir came back with the food things, freshly scrubbed from the river, she brought her father back too. Her father brought their two cows. Maaz settled the animals at the far end of the room, behind their bit of fencing, then he sank onto his straw bed by the wall. He didn't look at Ruel when he spoke to him.

'Go,' he said. 'Don't stay long. Don't go again.'

Ruel left without a word.

He took a few steps and stopped, breathing deeply. The fresh air always felt great when he came out of the smoky stink of his home – like drinking cool, fresh water – but there was something else good about those deep breaths this evening. He seemed to swell inside himself – to get bigger and bigger without any chance of ever bursting. He knew that he hadn't really won – he'd had to say he wouldn't see Zilla again – and even if he'd got his own way about this evening, it was Safir who'd sorted it out, not him – but at least he'd stood up for himself, he'd spoken up for what he thought was right, and that felt good – that felt like Hanan.

The village of Hazar had only one street and Ruel set off down it with big strides. It was an earth track and in summer it was baked hard; but it was only early spring now, and the mud was up to Ruel's ankles. The street ran east to west – out of the forest, through the village and back into the forest again. To the east, a day's journey by cart, was the town of Kiriath and Baron Azal's castle. To the west was the sea: but no one knew how far, or what was in between. Going west, the villagers kept the path clear as far as they needed into the forest, but beyond that it probably faded out to nothing. Hazar might even be the end of the road. That's how it felt anyway – no one ever came in from the west. To the north were the fields, hacked out of the forest so long ago no one could remember; to the south were the rocks and the river. Everything else was trees.

Up and down the street, the villagers were driving their animals home – mostly cattle, some pigs. Ruel nodded to them or said goodnight as they passed. They nodded back or said a word or two in reply. All that was normal, but there seemed to be something different about it this evening. Suddenly Ruel realised what it was – he was looking at his neighbours in a different way now – looking at their eyes – trying to read their thoughts. Did they really think the same way about him as they thought about Zilla? Were they starting to? *Would* they start to? Because his mother was right – Zilla *was* an outcast.

It wasn't just what she said. She didn't help herself by

the way she looked. Being old, she couldn't help having white hair – but did she have to make it into something that looked like a bush grown wild? And did she have to tie all those little strips of coloured cloth all over it? And did she have to wear such colourful clothes? Everyone else wore dull colours – browns, dirty looking blues and greens. But somehow, Zilla had learned the art of dyeing. No one knew what she used – berries or special roots that only she knew about – but she could make the most incredible *bright* colours. And she could never seem to stick to one colour for the rough gowns she wore: they were always sewn together from bits of every colour you could think of. She looked like a rainbow that had fallen out of the sky and landed in a tangled, mixed-up heap. Then there was the jewellery – not that any of it was real jewels, or gold, or even metal – all bits of stone or wood that she'd painted and strung round herself. You could hear her coming a mile off – she rattled.

Everyone thought she was mad – even wicked, although they never came out and said just how or why exactly. People were always making comments – not just the children, the grown-ups too. Whenever they wanted to make a mean joke about someone, it was always Zilla they picked on. Ruel realised he didn't want to be treated that way. He realised something else too – he might have stood up for himself at home just now, but he had never stood up for Zilla in the village. He might not have laughed at the jokes, but he'd never said they were wrong. He wasn't breathing quite so deeply, or feeling quite so good about himself by the time Zilla's cottage came in sight.

Only the miller and the blacksmith lived in a different style of house to Ruel's cottage. The rest lived in exactly the same kind of house – thatched, one room, straw beds round the walls, animals fenced off at the far end, everything else you owned hanging in bags from the beams where even someone Safir's height could bang their heads on them. Most of the places were the same size as Ruel's, some were smaller. Zilla's was the smallest of them all; and it was right on the western edge, where the track disappeared into the trees. In this twilight, you could easily miss it if you didn't know it was there. It was so small that the roof came down to the ground – like a tent. And the thatch was so old that it was green with all the things growing on it. It could have been a mound, Ruel thought – which made Zilla's home feel a bit like a burrow.

Ruel opened the door without knocking or calling, as he'd done hundreds of times before. Zilla knew it was him and didn't even look up. Her little fire was burning in its square stone enclosure in the middle of the tiny room, and she sat on her bit of log, staring deep into the flames.

'Come in, dearie,' she said, in her soft, dreamy voice. 'Come and sit down.'

Ruel sat beside her and kissed her dry old cheek. He'd no idea how old she was – just about the oldest in the village, that was for sure. She ruffled his hair and squeezed his hand for a moment. It was only then that she managed to tear her eyes away from the fire and look at him. She had big eyes, dark grey like a winter sky before it snows, and they always looked serious – even when she was making a joke. But Ruel knew there wouldn't be any jokes tonight.

'Now, have you eaten?' she said, starting to heave herself up off the log. 'If you just hang on a minute, I'll get you a nice—'

'No, Zilla – I've had something—'

'I've got some fruit pie, I could—'

'No really.'

Zilla's food – where she got it and how she cooked it – was as much of a mystery as the things she did with coloured cloth. Ruel didn't often get out of her cottage without some of it inside him. She seemed to have a need to feed people – and he supposed he was the only one who ever came near her these days to be fed. It was usually quite good food too – but different. He never asked what was in it.

It was rare for anyone not to feel hungry in Hazar, but tonight Ruel really didn't have any appetite.

'I can't stay long,' he said. Better to get it over with.

'Never mind, dear.' She patted his hand. 'Maybe another time.'

'There won't be another time.'

'Why's that, then, dearie? Are you going away somewhere?'

Ruel took a deep breath. 'There's been some trouble at home,' he said. And he told her about it all in a rush so she couldn't interrupt him.

She didn't say anything for a while when he'd finished. She sniffed a bit, and he knew she was crying. Those big grey eyes seemed to be made for staring or crying – she did each of them a lot, and Ruel found them both disturbing. Zilla was not an easy friend to have. Ruel could well have felt relieved that he wouldn't be seeing her again, but he didn't.

'They're right, dearie,' she said at last. 'You mustn't be cross with them. They're only doing what's best for you. I should have said it myself – I'm just a selfish old woman that should know better. Off you go now – it's good of them to let you come and tell me – off you go quickly now,' and she started prising herself off her log again as if she was going to see him out.

'No!' he said. 'Not yet.'

'You must do as your parents tell you, Ruel.'

'But what about Hanan? We haven't talked about Hanan.'

Zilla's eyes went suddenly soft and deep, as if the real Zilla wasn't on the bright surface of them any more but had fallen miles inside herself – as if the greyness of her eyes was made up of thick mist or cloud that you could fall through for ever. She sank back onto the log.

'I thought you'd want to talk,' Ruel said, softly. 'That's why I came.'

And so they went through it again – the story they'd shared since Ruel had first got to know her – since the day she'd dragged him out of the river. It had been a freezing winter's day, four years ago, and he'd been playing by the water. He had slipped on an icy stone and pitched straight in. The river was swollen and carried him off before anyone had seen what had happened – away downstream to the lonely spot where Zilla was pounding her washing. She had dragged him out and desperately tried to keep him alive. He was frozen stiff and she'd known that if he passed out he'd be dead. She'd hugged him and shook him and talked to him endlessly about everything she could think of. She'd held onto him with everything she'd got, and he'd lived. He remembered hardly any of it afterwards – apart from one story she had told – a story that had seemed to clutch onto him as Zilla had clutched him and dragged him out of the icy depths – the story of Hanan.

Zilla had got half way through telling it now when a furious banging at her door cut her short. Ruel opened it and found himself staring at Safir, standing in the moonlight.

'It's my sister,' he called to Zilla.

'Bring her in, dearie, bring her in – maybe *she'll* have some of my pie.'

'No, no,' said Safir. She was breathless from running and her eyes looked wild. 'You must come home quickly.'

'What is it?' Ruel asked.

'The Reaper – he's been seen in the forest – it's not safe to be out.'

Zilla's dreaminess went in an instant. 'Go on, dear,' she said, 'you must go straight away.'

Ruel went back to Zilla and hugged her tight.

'I'll miss you,' he said. 'I won't forget.'

Then Ruel and Safir were out in the night. It was quite dark now – the full moon making weird shadows everywhere. Ruel was furious at the danger his sister had been in.

'It's not safe for you to be out alone, if The Reaper's been seen,' he said – the darkness and danger turning his voice into a whisper. 'Why did Dad send you?'

'He didn't,' she hissed back. 'I was getting wood from the stack when I heard some men talking – they reckoned they'd just seen him in the forest – so I came for you straight away.'

'You idiot – what if he'd got *you*?'

'What if he'd got *you*? I wasn't going to let you walk home alone with him out there!'

'What if he gets both of us?'

'Come on then, let's run!'

Safir grabbed his hand and they pelted for the safety of home.

The glowing embers of the fire were just bright enough for Ruel to make out his brother's outline when Ezer poked him awake later that night. They shared a bed and often kneed or elbowed each other in their sleep, but this was a hard, persistent poke with the finger.

'Ruel – wake up!' Ezer whispered when he heard his brother grunt.

'What is it?'

'I can't get to sleep.'

'Why not?'

'I want to know who Hanan is.'

Suddenly Ruel was fully awake. The last evening rushed back into his mind – the argument with his father, the visit to Zilla, running home with Safir in the moonlight, the shouting when they'd got back because their parents hadn't known where Safir had gone, the stunned silence when she'd reported the sighting of The Reaper.

'Mum doesn't want me to tell you,' Ruel whispered, looking instinctively over to the dim shape of his parents, asleep by the opposite wall.

'That's why I want to know! Tell me, *please!*' Ezer was whispering too, but there was real desperation in his voice.

Ruel hesitated. What good had knowing about Hanan ever done anyone, he asked himself. It had made an outcast of Zilla and might make one of him if he went on about it to people. Much better to let it drop like everyone else in the village seemed to have done. Let it drop like a stone into icy water, never to be seen again. Ruel realised that he had been the same age as Ezer was now when he had fallen into the river – when he had first heard the story. He looked over to his parents again – no movement that he could make out in the dim light. His father was snoring. His mother's breath was lighter, but he knew it was the slow rhythm of sleep. Ezer was up on one elbow now, hanging over his brother.

'*Please!*' he hissed again.

Ruel pulled him down so that Ezer's ear was near his mouth.

'Have you ever heard of the King?' he whispered.

'Of course – he's in a fairy story,' Ezer replied, 'everybody knows that.'

'That's not what Hanan said,' Ruel told him. 'Hanan said he was a messenger from the King. Things were bad then – just like they are today – crops and animals were being taken – and people too, just like now – but Hanan said the King would come to sort it all out.'

'But who *was* Hanan? Where did he come from?'

'Nobody knew. Zilla said he came from the east, beyond Kiriath. She said he was a huge man, with a great bush of hair. He wore animal skins. She said he looked like a great forest bear.'

'Did she really know him?'

'They all knew him – all the grown-ups in the village.'

'Why don't they talk about him, then? Why did Mum say he ought to be forgotten?'

'They all fell out with him.'

'Why?'

'Because they wouldn't be patient. That's what Zilla says. He promised them the King would come to help them and the King didn't show up, so they got cross with Hanan – said he'd told them lies. He travelled round all the villages in the forest, telling everyone all about the King and how he was going to make everything different, and they all got really excited. They started planning for the future. They held village councils to work out how to organise things when the King came to take charge and everything was all right again. And they all got fired up about joining the King to fight for their freedom. They weren't going to let themselves be walked all over any more – they were going to stand up for themselves, with the King to help them. But then the King never showed up.'

'What happened to Hanan?'

'Nobody knows for sure. One day he got an invitation to go and visit Baron Azal in Kiriath, to tell him all about the King. Zilla says he didn't want to go but it was the sort of invitation you can't refuse – ten of Azal's soldiers brought it. So he went to Kiriath, and he's never been seen since.'

'When did all this happen?'

'Zilla says it was a couple of years before Safir was born.'

'That's a long time.' Ezer seemed to think for a while. 'And the King still hasn't come.'

'No – but Zilla says we have to be *patient* – we have to keep *believing*. She says he *will* come one day, just like Hanan said. That's why everyone hates her. They think it's stupid to hope. They think it's better to learn to accept things the way they are. They're *glad* that Hanan's gone, and they don't want to hear about him or think about him any more.'

There was a long silence and Ruel thought his brother had gone to sleep. The embers were nearly dead now, and Ruel couldn't see Ezer at all. Then there was a rustle in the straw and Ruel could feel Ezer's breath on his face as his brother leaned over him.

'I do,' Ezer whispered. 'I want to think about him.'

chapter two

ighteen cottages, a mill and the blacksmith's, then there were the rocks by the river. That made plenty of places to hide in Hazar – and that was without going into the trees, or the fields, or down near old Zilla's. Mind you, no one would dream of going to hide down by Zilla's, and her cottage wasn't even counted in the eighteen. But then there were places in the village itself you'd be pretty wary about going near. The blacksmith's, for instance. Halak the blacksmith was not a man to mess around with – built like a mountain, with a bald shiny head and eyes like tiny glass beads. He didn't talk much, just growled and waved his hammer at the children – or anyone else who annoyed him. Sometimes he threw things. Then there was Machir the miller – a miserable little man that no one liked but everyone had to deal with. He was the only one in Hazar with any money and he always suspected that anyone nosing around his mill was trying to steal it. As for the fields, everyone got cross if the children started running around there, and anyway, there wasn't much cover for a good game of hide and seek at this time of year. And the trees – well, they were fine if you wanted to spend all day over your game. Ten strides into the forest and any child could be lost to even a grown-up hunter for hours.

Today, however, there was another reason for not going into the forest to play. Last night's rumours were still flying about in the village. Had those men really seen The Reaper? No one was taking any chances. All the children had had strict instructions from their parents not to go near the trees – and for once, no one had the slightest thought of disobeying. Some of them weren't even too keen on playing the game at all. For over twenty years the children of the forest villages had had a special name for hide and seek – they called it 'Pig's Head'. The game was a grim reminder of what the menace in the forest was all about. What life in Hazar and the rest of the forest villages was all about, for that matter. They were all hiding away, hoping they were safe, dreading the time a pig's head on a stick told the villagers The Reaper was calling for his dues, dreading the moment they might be picked out. But there was one big difference between the game and real life. If you were found when you were playing 'Pig's Head' at least you had a chance of survival. If you could beat the chaser back to the starting point – in Hazar, that was the tall stone by the mill – then you'd escaped. But if the real-life Reaper called you, that was it – no escape, no chances, you'd had it.

It was Ruel who'd thought of playing 'Pig's Head' that morning. By the time they started to bump into each other and gang together, all the children in Hazar had heard the news that The Reaper had been seen, and they were quiet, edgy – kicking stones and not knowing what to do. When Ruel had suggested the game, they'd all looked at him as if he was mad for a minute. Then a few of them started to get the point.

'Sure, it doesn't scare me.'

'Me neither.'

'Yeah – let's play 'Pig's Head'.'

Soon everyone had said their bit about it being all right with them, and then they all felt better. They drew lots to see who was going to chase. Then they were ready to get started.

Just at that moment Safir appeared at her cottage door, carrying some scraps for the hens. She wasn't really supposed to play with the children any more, but like everyone else, she was on edge and needed company.

When she saw what they were doing, she scattered the scraps, snatched up the hem of her dress, and raced across to the starting stone. Ruel was going to chase and put his hands over his eyes. He rested his head against the stone – it was just as tall as he was – and started to count. There were screams like the seagulls made when the scarers went running at them with their wooden clappers to drive them off the crops, and the youngsters scattered round the village.

Just running wild and screeching like that was good. Safir felt the air streaming past her face as she ran – tugging her hair out behind her like a banner – and she let out a long high whoop. Run – run like the wind. That was the thing to do when you were all wound up inside. It wasn't running like running away – that made your heart thump too fast and your eyes bulge out like a rabbit's. No, this was running to show you were alive, strong, full of power. Her feet drove into the ground and her legs launched her in long bouncing strides. She was alive. She was invincible. She could fly! She didn't want to stop. She went to the very edge of the village – to the last cottage before you got to Zilla's. She had just flopped down behind the wood stack there when she heard her brother's voice ringing round the village.

'Coming, ready or not!'

It was tiring work. Every time Ruel found someone he had to sprint back to the stone, then set off hunting again. But gradually he picked them off, and most of them got caught – he was one of the fastest runners in the village. He still hadn't caught Safir, though. But then, he knew where she was. By the time he'd searched half way down the street, he knew exactly which cottage she was hiding by, and exactly where. Not that he could see her – she was good at hiding – but he'd always been able to know where she was. It was a sort of feeling. Yes, he knew she was hiding behind the wood stack at the last cottage in the village.

And that was good, because he'd wanted to save her till last anyway.

Safir had already been found by the owner of the end cottage when the woman had gone to her stack for some wood. They'd had a laugh about Safir playing children's games, but the woman's son, Chilion, was still a big baby, so his mother reckoned, and he was twenty-one, so she wasn't cross with Safir. But then people were always more likely to have a laugh with Safir than to shout at her. The woman looked up the street and reported on Ruel's progress, then left Safir to hide in peace.

Soon after, Safir heard the squawk of a disturbed hen at the side of the cottage. But she knew already that Ruel was creeping carefully down the back wall. She could feel him there. The wood stack was at the far end of the cottage, and as Ruel edged down the back wall, Safir moved silently round to the front. But she didn't seem to want the start this gave her. When Ruel turned the corner of the house, there she was not two steps away, waiting for him. They stood smiling at each other for a moment. Then Safir snatched her dress free of her feet and spun away from him.

'Go!' she shouted, and sprinted off up the street with her brother tearing after her.

Maybe Ruel was tired from so much running already whilst Safir had been resting, or maybe Safir was just so full of life that day that nothing could catch her; but whatever the reason, Ruel stayed a stride behind her all the way up the street. By the time they swung round the end cottage he'd made up a pace, and they launched down the grassy slope towards the mill, side by side.

All the children were on their feet chanting, '*Safir! Safir! Safir!*'

Machir the miller had poked his head out of his door and was shouting something, but no one could hear him. Brother and sister threw themselves at the starting stone together. No one knew who'd won, and no one cared. The pair of them lay on their backs staring at the clouds passing by – pale grey against pale blue – their lungs feeling like they were being rubbed by sandpaper on the inside with every breath.

But as soon as the next chaser started to count and the children scattered, Ruel and Safir were on their feet again and jogging away together. They didn't discuss it, but they knew exactly where they were going – Halak the blacksmith's. One good thing about hiding at the blacksmith's or the miller's was that the chaser probably wouldn't dare nose around too much to look for you there. They'd have plenty of time to rest.

The bellows were roaring like a dragon and they could hear the steady clang of Halak's hammer battering the glowing metal into the shape he wanted it. No wonder his arms looked as thick as tree trunks, bang, bang, banging like that, day after day, week after week. The children might have been frightened of Halak, but they had plenty of admiration for him too. It was pretty amazing to see a person built like that. He was the nearest thing they had to a superman in Hazar. But even he was scared of The Reaper – the deadly 'chaser' who might, even now, be creeping around in the forest.

Ruel and Safir tucked themselves into the corner made by the big stone chimney and the wall of the smithy. The warmth of the stone, heated by the furnace inside, was very welcome – the spring air was cold when you stopped moving.

'We'll be all right here,' Ruel said. 'He won't dare come near Halak's.'

They were quiet for a while, getting their breath back, listening to the mighty sounds of the smithy, and catching the odd shout and scream from the game.

'I wish there was somewhere The *Reaper* didn't dare

come near,' Safir said after a while.

Ruel hesitated for a moment. 'Maybe there is,' he said.

His sister looked at him. 'Not that I've ever heard of.'

Ruel seemed almost embarrassed. 'I bet he daren't go near the King's castle,' he said.

Safir laughed. 'He'd have to know where it is before he could be scared of it.'

Ruel met her eyes, trying to read her expression. She looked away.

'You don't think it exists, do you?' he asked at last.

'I didn't say that.'

'But you're thinking it.'

'I don't know what to think.'

'Hanan said—'

His sister cut him off, sounding irritated. 'You don't know *what* Hanan said – only what Zilla's told you. Anyway, Mum said you had to let all that drop.'

It always made them unhappy to argue but Ruel couldn't just leave it.

'I can't stand the way no one wants to talk about *anything*,' he said. 'It's like The Reaper. Why won't anyone talk about him? They won't even give him his proper name – he's a *man* – he's just a man – his name's Zabad. Why do we have to call him The Reaper all the time?'

'What difference does it make *what* we call him?'

'Don't you see? If you give him a silly name, it's like he's some kind of monster that you can't do anything about. If you give him his proper name, you remember he's just a man.'

Safir considered this for a while. She watched a woman taking washing down to the river, a man leading one of his cows away up to the road – ordinary people getting on with their ordinary lives.

'Perhaps people don't *want* to remember,' she said at last.

Now it was Ruel's turn to be irritated. 'They don't want to think at *all*,' he said. 'That's the point – talking means thinking and they don't want to think about any of this. They just want it to go away. But it *won't* go away unless someone *does* something about it.'

'What *can* we do?' his sister asked.

They looked at each other, and both of them knew that if Ruel answered that, they'd be into talking about Hanan again. Ruel clammed up and rubbed earth between his fingers for something to do.

'They won't even talk about what happens when Zabad comes,' he said after a while. 'It's as if they want to pretend it's not happening.'

'He takes people away,' Safir said, coldly. 'No one tries to hide that. They get chosen and they get taken away. What else is there to say?'

'Plenty – what happens to them *after* they get taken away? That's what we need to talk about. Have you ever tried asking? That's the quickest way I know to get rid of a grown-up. Just ask them what happens to people The Reaper takes away and they'll be at the other end of the village before you can blink.'

'What's the *point* of asking?' Safir said, impatiently. 'Everyone knows the answer.'

Ruel replied very slowly, counting off the points he was making on his fingers. 'If you ask questions, people have to *talk* about things. If they *talk* about things they have to *think* about them. If people would only think about what's really going on here, they might actually *do* something about it.'

A shout broke them off. They looked up and saw the chaser in their game waving at them from a mound down by the river. As Ruel had said, he didn't dare come near the blacksmith's but he'd got himself to the only place you could see their little hiding place from a safe distance. Now it was a sprint back to the starting stone, and from where he was, the chaser had quite a lead. He was one of the young teenagers who really ought to have had better things to do, so he should have been able to beat them easily; but he was one of those boys whose arms and legs seem to do a lot of flapping around without achieving very much, so the race was definitely on.

It was great to run together, not against each other but as a team this time. And Ruel and Safir soon realised they could relax and enjoy it – the boy was such a hopeless runner that they would pass him way before the stone, even without going flat out. The boy looked over his shoulder. His face was like a beetroot with the effort and he could see that he was going to be beaten. Brother and sister swept towards him like a pair of deer in full flight. Then the boy did something that wasn't in the rules. He turned round and blocked Safir's path. It was so quick and unexpected that Ruel had gone way past them before he realised what had happened, and pulled up. He was going to run back, but what he saw stopped him dead. The boy was holding Safir by her upper arms, but he didn't seem to be gripping her; and instead of struggling to get free she was holding his arms too, as if she was steadying herself. They were just looking at each other and not moving.

At that moment, Safir's mother appeared on the scene. She'd been sweeping up outside their cottage and had seen what was going on. Now she came charging down the little slope towards them. She still had her broom in her hand and when she got to Safir she jammed it between her and the boy, and used it to drive her daughter back towards the cottage.

'*That's* why you shouldn't be playing with the children any more,' she said. 'You're *not* a child now, Safir, and you can't act like one. You're a grown-up woman and you should be doing grown-up work.'

Naama's voice trailed off as she and Safir disappeared into their cottage. Ruel was puzzled. She might have been waving her broom about, but his mother hadn't really seemed cross with Safir. He almost thought he'd caught a bit of a laugh in her voice.

The scene broke up the game. The children had got bored with it anyway by now. Everyone drifted off in ones and twos. The older ones took the hint from what Safir's mother had said and went looking for something more useful to do. The gangly boy hung around for a bit, looking at Safir's cottage and then at Ruel, as if he might be going to say something, then he went away too. That left only Ruel. Machir the miller came out and started shuffling towards him, looking like a ghost with flour all over his clothes and face and hair. The children were scared of Machir, but Ruel had the feeling Machir was scared of *them* – he never seemed to come out and take them on when there was a bunch of them, only when he could catch someone on their own. He started blathering on about showing respect and not using his estate as a playground. 'Estate'! It was a bit of grass beside his mill that didn't even belong to him as far as Ruel, or anyone else, was concerned. Ruel turned his back on the man and walked down to the river.

The rocks were really big. They looked as if they'd been thrown down beside the water by a giant centuries ago. The children liked to make up stories about them. And the old folks too. They were as high as a cottage – dark grey, gritty rock, good to climb on and a good place to sit and look at the river. That's what Ruel did now. The water wasn't far off the colour of the rocks, and he watched it rushing past, full of spring rain. It was beautiful, powerful, and it had nearly killed him once. Being close to it helped him go very still inside himself and think.

After a while Ruel went off downstream to the place where Zilla did her washing. She wasn't there. He knew she wouldn't be. It wasn't the right day. He sat where she usually sat and looked at the stones she used to pound her clothes. He thought about scratching a message on one of them. Apart from the miller, Zilla was the only person in the village who could read and write, and she'd taught Ruel too. He got a sharp stone to write with and tossed it from hand to hand, but in the end he dropped it into the water. It wouldn't be right. Not after his promise. He could hear the sounds of birds calling in the trees. The dim green light seemed to say, 'Come on in, make yourself at home, wander round, see what you can find.' It was *his* forest – his *home*, and there was no way he was going to let Zabad scare him out of it. He wouldn't go far, but he was going to do what the green light told him.

It was the middle of the afternoon before Ruel got back. And as soon as he came out of the trees and headed for the cottages he knew there was something wrong. All the noises were wrong. He couldn't hear anything to do with work, just a lot of shouting. Then there was some screaming. He could see that the grassy space by the mill, Machir's 'estate' as he'd called it, was crowded with people, and straight away he knew what it was. If there had to be a village meeting about anything, that's where everyone always went. And with Zabad on the prowl there was only one reason they'd all be meeting. The Reaper had called for a sacrifice, and they were meeting to choose who it was going to be.

By the sound of all the screaming and wailing going on, the choice had already been made.

A horrible feeling, like something squashing his heart, suddenly sent Ruel racing towards the scene. He arrived just in time to see two men leading the latest sacrifice up the bank towards the village street – next stop, the trees. There was a huge fallen trunk a ten-minute walk into the forest – this was where The Reaper would collect his victim. Ruel saw at once what his heart had known already – the victim was Safir.

Many of the women were wailing, Ruel's mother amongst them – a wordless, animal howl. Into the middle of the din, booming like a thunderclap, came a single word.

'NO!'

It was Ruel's voice, and as he shouted he crashed through the crowd, sending grown men and women staggering from the impact. He'd charged right through the lot of them before he was finally brought to a halt. Huge arms reached out and hands as broad as spades had hold of him. It was Halak. Ruel kicked out at the blacksmith's legs and punched anything he could reach, but there was no shifting him. Ruel looked up into the man's face ready to spit, but something stopped him. Halak's tiny glass-bead eyes were wet with tears.

Ruel saw his father standing a step behind the blacksmith. Maaz looked as if he'd taken a battering – his shoulders were drooping, his knees were shaky and his head hung low.

'Dad!' Ruel shouted. 'They can't do it! Quick! You've got to stop them! We don't send children – it's grown-ups we send! Tell them! Tell them!'

He was wriggling furiously, bruising himself in Halak's grip, pointing desperately towards the little group of three, by now disappearing into the forest.

'She's not a child!' Maaz roared.

His face had snapped up and he was glaring at Ruel in a way that shocked him. His father looked stark staring mad.

'She's not a child any more!' Maaz shouted at his son. 'When we drew lots, she had to go in with everyone else. They all said so!'

He waved his arms furiously at the crowd, and everyone looked away – at the ground, at the sky, anywhere but at Maaz.

Ruel went still, and Halak let him go. The boy seemed dazed. He came close to his father and started talking quickly and quietly, as if he was sharing a secret.

'We'll have to go after her,' he said. 'Everyone needs to get a weapon – axes, billhooks, staves, knives – we've got plenty – Halak can lead us.'

His father's head had drooped again.

'No,' he said, so softly that only Ruel could hear.

'But Dad, we've got to.'

'No.'

'There's still time, Dad, if we're quick – if we go now.'

'No, son.'

'We can *do* it, Dad – we've *got* to. We can't just *leave* her.'

Gradually his father's lungs had been filling. 'I've told you – NO!' he shouted.

He had his son by the shoulders in a grip that felt much fiercer than Halak's.

'You can't mean it!' Ruel shouted back. 'Why? Just tell me *why* we can't do anything to save her!'

'You know as well as I do – The Reaper must have a prisoner or we'll all be destroyed – the lots have been drawn – it was Safir. She has to save us.'

'*Save* us? Save us for *what*? To be picked off one by one? We might as well be destroyed, the lot of us, and have done with it.'

There was a lot of angry muttering going on in the crowd by now, but it wasn't clear who the anger was against. Ruel sensed his father's grip slacken and he suddenly twisted himself free.

'Well if *you're* not going, *I* will!' he shouted, and took off towards the trees.

He never got further than his first stride. Before his toes could dig in the turf for a second one, his head seemed to explode.

When Ruel opened his eyes, he was staring at the clouds crossing the late afternoon sky – darkening grey against darkening blue. He could smell the earth close to his face, and he could smell his mother. He realised she was kneeling next to him, holding his hand, and that he was lying on the ground. He levered himself painfully up on one elbow, and made out the shape of his father crouching down a few paces away, watching him. Everyone else had gone.

In the instant Ruel had made for the trees, Maaz had swung his thick, forester's arm and laid his son out with the back of his hand.

Chapter Three

E verything seemed upside down. Maaz never thought twice about what happened when he lost his temper – but now he wanted to say sorry to his son for hitting him. Ruel could tell how Maaz was feeling in the days after Safir was taken. He could read it from the lines that always stayed wrinkled up on his father's forehead – the way his eyes kept sliding off to look at the ground, and his big, strong body drooped and didn't seem to know what to do with itself. Normally Ruel would have been glad to see Maaz so uncomfortable – these days he spent most of his time trying to get one over on his father. But Ruel's own feelings were upside down too – all he wanted to do now was tell Maaz it didn't matter.

Neither of them said anything though – to each other, or to anyone. Day followed day in almost complete silence – just the words they needed to get the jobs done. And that was how it always was after someone had been taken. No one talked about it – in the family, or in the village. It was just what Ruel had been explaining to his sister the day she'd been taken – people didn't want to think, so they didn't talk. Silence was the rule. So the biggest shock of all came to Ruel when even that got turned upside down.

'There's going to be a meeting,' Maaz told his family one morning, about ten days after they'd lost Safir. 'Everybody has to be there. Jarib's called it. He says even Zilla has to come.'

It was amazing. A wild hope came bubbling up inside Ruel – they were going to talk! Perhaps they might *do* something at last! Without thinking he turned to share this incredible idea with the only person in his family he ever *did* share his ideas with – but Safir wasn't there. He'd lost count of the number of times in the last few days when he'd done that. Whenever it happened, it left him feeling as weak and sore as if he'd been in a fight that had lasted all morning. His father hitting him really *was* nothing compared to what had come after – in his heart, Ruel felt as if he'd been beaten up a dozen times a day ever since.

The villagers looked like sleepwalkers as they made their way to the meeting place – the miller's 'estate'. It was a misty morning, and the people of Hazar were silent as ghosts. They moved as if they hardly had enough weight in them to keep their feet on the ground. In ones and twos and family groups, they settled in a ragged circle on the grass. It was damp and uncomfortable, but they didn't seem to care. The children were there too. It would be a brave child who ever said anything at one of these village assemblies, but they were expected to be there. Ruel took Ezer onto his knee. Normally, Ezer would have wriggled off straight away and thumped his brother – he wasn't a baby any more. But now he settled against Ruel's chest without complaining. Ruel squinted through the haze. Maaz was right – Zilla was there, right at the back, at the other side of the circle. He badly wanted to make some sign to her but didn't. She wasn't looking anyway. She seemed to be staring at Jarib.

Jarib was sitting on a special stone that was brought out for him whenever there was one of these meetings. It wasn't a throne. Jarib wasn't like a king or a chief. He sat in the circle like everyone else. It was so that people could see him, and he could see everyone. His job was to start off the meeting and tell people when they could speak and when they'd gone on long enough, and to say when the meeting was over. It was also his job to tell the meeting what it had decided. They never voted on things – Jarib just listened to everything everyone said – or didn't say – and got a feel for what it all amounted to, then he put it into words. Sometimes he would tell the meeting that they hadn't decided anything at all. People didn't have to accept what Jarib said – they could argue with him, but they hardly ever did.

Nobody was very clear about when Jarib had started doing this job in the meetings. Even Zilla didn't seem to be able to remember. To most of the grown-up villagers Jarib had seemed like an old man when they were children. Now he seemed so old to everybody that he was like something that had always been there. He was like the mountain far away to the north – the only thing to break the ring of trees that was their horizon. But Jarib was a fine-looking old man. He sat up straight and strong as a tree trunk. And he still had all his hair and teeth – which was more than you could say about a lot of the men in Hazar. Both of them were shiny white. His hair was long – halfway down his back. Zilla had once told Ruel that long ago all the men used to wear their hair like that. And he had a beard – that used to be the fashion too, apparently, many years ago. It was a long, silky beard, reaching down to his chest. The children always wanted to stroke it, and sometimes he let them, because he wasn't a scary old man – or crotchety. His eyes were the best part about him – brilliant blue – not watery or bloodshot. They were always serious, but they made you feel good when you looked into them.

Jarib's eyes were never jolly. They were serious – ordinary serious or sad serious. Today they were sad serious in a way Ruel had never seen before. When everyone was gathered, the old man took his time looking round before he started to talk. At last he pressed down hard on the thick staff he had in his hand and heaved himself onto his feet.

'Friends,' he started off, 'this is not the way we do things. We don't meet to discuss our suffering. We suffer and we keep silent. Every harvest we take our crops to The Reaper: he leaves us just enough to keep alive – and yet we stay silent. When our animals are fattened, the best of them go to The Reaper and there is hardly enough meat left to put muscle on the bodies of our children – yet we stay silent. But all this is nothing. Worst of all, every year, The Reaper comes to us to demand a life. We draw lots, send our sacrifice, and *still* we are silent.'

Jarib paused for a moment. He didn't sit down – which was the sign for the discussion to start – but one of the young men jumped up. It was Chilion – the one whose mother thought he was still a baby. Maybe he was trying to prove he was a man, Ruel thought, being first to speak in the assembly.

'What else can we *do*?' he shouted. 'If it was just The Reaper it would be different. Or if he was working for an ordinary boss – someone we could fight and stand a chance against. But what can we do against The Reaper's master?'

There was a lot of muttering – people agreeing. Chilion sat down. He looked pleased with himself.

Jarib was still on his feet. 'Our young friend speaks the truth,' he said, bowing slightly to Chilion. 'The crops, the cattle, and the people go to Zabad's master, The Dragon – and because we believe we are helpless against such a monster there seems nothing more to say. And yet for days, in spite of that, I have sensed you *want* to talk about this latest loss. I am puzzled. I ask myself what has changed, and I find only this – before, when a victim has been taken one family grieves and the rest of Hazar rejoices.'

There was muttering again – but this time it was hard to tell its mood.

'Oh yes, my friends, in your secret hearts you have

rejoiced each time the victim was not from your family. But today *no one* rejoices, *all* grieve, because when we lost Safir we *all* lost someone we love. Friends, I feel it is *this* that makes you want to talk. Now you will show me if my feeling is right.'

Jarib sat down and waited.

Ruel looked disgusting. He had grease all over himself. It was all over his hands and his face – right up to his ears. It was shining in the light from his campfire. He tore like an animal at the rabbit he'd caught and cooked – but then, he *was* hungry. He wasn't dirty by the time he'd finished, though – he'd sucked his hands clean, then scrubbed them round his face and licked and sucked them again. It wasn't surprising he was hungry – it had taken him ages to catch the rabbit and he'd been out all day in the forest, ever since he'd slipped away from the big assembly in Hazar that morning.

Jarib had been right. The villagers *did* want to talk. The old man had had a hard job keeping order as speaker after speaker jumped up to say their piece. There was fury, passion, wild words – words of love. Jarib had been right about that too. Ruel had got excited – the whole village seemed to be in the same pain that he was. This *was* different, just like Jarib had said. Ruel had never known anything like it. It seemed like what Zilla had described when Hanan had been around. Old Zilla even got to speak about Hanan and the sort of thing he'd said they ought to do, and nobody shouted her down. There even seemed to be some people who agreed with her. Surely now something would be done. The talk went on and on.

Then something strange seemed to happen. Ruel

couldn't put his finger on exactly when, but at some point the fury seemed to start leaking away – when people got up to speak there was more of a whine in their voices. When everyone shouted out to show they agreed with whoever was on their feet, it sounded more like a moan than a roar. The things that were said started to sound desperate rather than full of passion. And still no one was suggesting actually *doing* anything. Ruel went cold inside. He didn't need to wait around to know how it would end up. He knew that when the talking finished Jarib would tell the village it had decided nothing. The mist had closed in around the ring of villagers. Ruel slipped silently away, collected a knife and fire flints from his cottage, and sprinted into the trees. No one saw him go.

A knife – not even a good one at that: he'd gutted the rabbit with it, but that was about all it was fit for. Not much of a weapon to go off on a quest with. Still, it was worth looking after, since it was all he had. Ruel wiped it carefully on some leaves after he'd finished with the rabbit, and put it down where he could see it, the blade shining in the firelight. He was frightened. He couldn't hide it from himself. Every time there was a crackle from the fire, or any other kind of noise, his eyes scoured the clearing where he was camped. Not that it did much good straining his eyes – it was night – pitch black – and the forest was so thick you could only just about squeeze a horse between the trees. That's if you *had* a horse, which he didn't – horses were for rich people. Of course, this wasn't the first time he'd been in the forest at night. He'd been out a few times with Maaz. But tonight was different. This time he was on his own – and no one had a clue where he was.

If he'd eaten like an animal, he moved like one too. He was just thinking of bedding down when suddenly, before he knew he was doing it, he leaped to his feet, knife in hand. He stood there quivering, his mind catching up with the sudden instinctive reaction to danger. His heart was hammering and he was staring at a point on the far side of the clearing. The light from the fire was just strong enough to catch the shape of a man between the trees. Ruel had no idea what had made him leap up, or how long the man had been there. Since he'd been old enough to understand anything, Maaz had trained him to pick up the tiniest sounds almost without thinking about it and know what they were. But apart from the crackling of the fire, Ruel hadn't heard a thing.

Neither of them moved or made a sound. The man seemed patient – as if he could wait a long time – perhaps he already had. Ruel realised it was down to him to make the first move and he beckoned with his free hand. He still kept the knife up though – hoping it looked as if he meant business. The man came slowly out into the clearing. His hands were loose by his sides where they could be seen – open and empty. As he came nearer the light Ruel could see he was wearing an old leather jerkin – all cracked and wrinkled as if he'd worn it to the end of the world and back. It didn't look as if he had any weapons on him. Ruel backed up a bit and put the little fire between them. The flames made a strange effect, lighting the man from below as he came nearer. He had long dark hair and his face was thin, sunken. His body was thin too, but it looked wiry and strong. Ruel had come across men like this before – crafty men who lived on their own out in the woods – cunning and dangerous. But there was something different about this man – something about the eyes. Ruel let his knife arm drop to his side and made a sign for the stranger to sit down. If it had come to a fight, he knew he wouldn't have stood a chance anyway.

'I haven't got any food,' Ruel warned.

'That's not what I've come for,' the stranger replied softly, settling himself by the fire.

'What are you doing here, then?'

'I saw your fire,' he explained. 'And you? What are you doing so far in the forest at night?'

Ruel sized him up for a minute – narrow, calm face; dark eyes, steady and deep; long powerful-looking fingers hanging relaxed as he rested his wrists on his drawn up knees. He didn't look like a man from any of the forest villages – and his accent was strange too. But it was good – he liked it. The question was, could he trust the man? But then again, what was there to trust him with? Not much when it came down to it – a dream really, that was all. And it had started to feel like a pretty foolish dream too, as he'd been sitting there tearing away at his rabbit, and jumping at every hiss from the fire.

'I'm on a quest,' he told him, without much confidence.

'A quest?' The man seemed to chew on the word. 'A quest must have a purpose. What are you searching for, my friend?'

A long pause.

'The King,' Ruel muttered at last, and he thought his voice sounded like Ezer's when he was owning up to something stupid he'd done.

The man just stared at him, and Ruel waited for him to burst out laughing. But he didn't. He seemed to be thinking seriously.

'The King?' he said. 'No one's seen a king in this land for years – a lifetime or more. You might come across a rambling old man who claims his mother saw one when she was a girl – that's about all. What makes you think there still *is* a King?'

'Or ever was one,' Ruel added. 'That's what some people say.'

'But not you? You think there is a King to be found?'

'There's got to be!'

'Why?'

'Because we need him!'

'Is that a reason?' the man asked, gently.

Ruel poked around at the fire. It was going out. He scraped together a few sticks and started to arrange them. The man helped, and between them they soon got the flames dancing again but there was no way the wood was going to last the night out. Ruel was past caring, and just sat staring at the bright shapes of the flames. He was tired too – exhausted. He didn't really notice the man get up and go, and he couldn't have said how long he was away. He heard him come back though – even in the state he was in, he still went for his knife. But as soon as he saw who it was he relaxed. Strangely he felt safe. The man put down an armful of branches – enough to see them through the night.

'*Why* do you need the King?' the stranger asked, settling down again by the fire.

'How long have you got?'

'As long as it takes to tell me.'

And so Ruel told him all about it – The Dragon, Zabad, the payment of crops, animals – people. How nobody seemed to be able to do anything about it. He even went into all the business about Hanan. He told him about Zilla, and the argument with his father. He told him everything – all except the one thing that was more important than any of the rest. But the man seemed to know he'd missed something out.

'Go on,' he prompted, when Ruel finally stopped talking.

Ruel looked at him hard for a moment.

'The Dragon got my sister,' he said at last. His voice was very small because it hurt to say it. 'That's what did it – I had to go. Someone's got to do something. The King's our only hope – someone's got to find him.'

'But where?'

Ruel looked at the stranger again to see if he was making fun of him. He wasn't – it was a genuine question. But it was a question there was no answer to. Zilla had never come up with one anyway – because, for all his fine words, Hanan had never come up with one either.

The silence lengthened, and Ruel felt that he had to say something. 'He lives in a castle made out of white stones,' he said, at last, closing his eyes to picture what he was describing. 'The best white there is – white as the clouds. It's right on top of a really high mountain, but the mountain's all covered with grass – soft grass, with flowers in it – red, blue, yellow – all kinds – and it's easy to climb. There's an easy path all the way, and you never get out of breath. And it's warm – even right at the top where there's usually snow on mountains – this one's just grass and really warm sunshine. Then when you get to the top the walls just look as if they go on for miles, right up into the sky. There's hundreds of turrets, and they've all got gold roofs, like tents, pointy at the top, with great big flags flapping out from them – red and blue and gold. Inside, the King sits in a room as big as a field where he has his banquets, and there's tapestries all over the walls with pictures of all his battles on them. Then there's his knights – a hundred of them – the bravest in all the world – all sitting round him in golden armour with great big swords and shields laid out in front of them, ready for battle the moment the King gives the word.'

Ruel stopped – broken off by a yawn that made his jaws crack. He was sitting with his knees pulled up, and he put his forehead on them to rest for a moment. Slowly the pictures in his mind began to lose their brightness. Thick mist swirled around them. They got smaller and darker, then faded into blackness. A while later, the man heard the rough steady breathing that told him the boy was deep in sleep. The stranger smiled, then went off to the edge of the clearing. A horse was standing there between the trees – completely still and silent. Ruel had never even noticed it. There were several bundles tied to the horse's saddle. The man undid one of them and pulled out a couple of rough woollen blankets. He got Ruel into a comfortable position and covered him up, then banked the fire for the night. When everything was sorted, he sat down cross-legged and draped the other blanket round his shoulders. He stared deep into the glowing fire.

❧

A forest is a noisy place at dawn. Ruel woke up to the din of the birds and the first light of a new day. He stretched and swore under his breath at the pain in his aching body. He felt as if someone had been kicking him all night long. He could smell wood burning, and heard the crackle of flames. There was the stranger, still sitting cross-legged by the fire, but he'd obviously been busy – the fire was mended after the night, and beside it was a loaf of dark-coloured bread and a leather drinking bottle.

'Come and have breakfast,' the man said.

When they'd finished, the stranger brought his horse into the middle of the clearing and packed the blankets away in the bundle on its saddle. Ruel just stared – he'd been surprised enough that the man had been able to creep up without being heard last night, but a horse as well – that was impossible! He couldn't work out how the man even came to *own* a horse in the first place – he didn't look much more than a beggar. And this wasn't just any old horse. Ruel could tell it was top quality. Maybe the man was a thief. The stranger saw Ruel staring, but he didn't say anything. When he was ready he wished Ruel success with his quest, and mounted up. Ruel noticed how easily he swung into the saddle – how naturally he sat in it. Suddenly, he didn't look like a beggar at all.

With a nudge so small you could hardly see it, the stranger set his horse walking.

'Why don't you come with me?' he called, over his shoulder.

Ruel was confused. 'Where are you going?' he asked.

The man didn't reply, but kept on walking his horse slowly towards the trees.

'I don't even know your name?'

He stopped the horse and turned in the saddle.

'Baladan will do. And yours?'

'Ruel.'

'Will you join me, Ruel?'

'But I've got to find the King.'

Baladan moved his horse on again. 'As you will,' he replied.

Ruel was confused. What did Baladan mean? Was he saying, 'You will find the King,' or 'You will find him with *me*,' or 'Please yourself'? Ruel stared after him and couldn't work it out. The spring sun was up now, striking low and sharp over the trees, and just as the man and his horse were about to disappear into their shadows, a blinding flash of light exploded in the clearing. Even as it was happening, Ruel knew what it was – the sun had caught something metal in the baggage on the horse – simple as that – but it seemed as if a fireball was bursting round his head. He was completely dazzled. His eyes were burning and he covered them with his arm. The whole forest seemed to erupt with whirring wings and screaming birds. Then quick as it came, the light was gone. Everything went absolutely still and silent.

Baladan was moving between the first trees now and Ruel saw what had caught the light. A flap of cloth had come loose from a long bundle hanging straight down from the horse's saddle. It showed the gilded hilt of what was obviously a battle sword. It swayed gently with the movement of the horse, giving a last twinkle as Baladan and his horse faded silently away amongst the trees.

Now it was Ruel's turn to get ready to leave. Not that that took much doing. He picked up the heel of the loaf that Baladan had left and stuffed it inside his shirt, stuck his knife in his belt and kicked out the fire. He scuffed plenty of damp earth over it to make sure it would do no damage, then stood still and looked round the clearing. Where? The question hadn't gone away. If he closed his eyes, he could still see the castle he'd described by the campfire as clear as day, but he hadn't the faintest idea if it existed anywhere outside his head, and if it did where he would find it. To be honest, he couldn't even work out for certain which way he'd got into this clearing the night before.

There was only one direction he knew for sure. Suddenly, as if someone had shouted 'Go!' in a race, he started to run. He ran full speed for the spot where Baladan and his horse had disappeared into the trees.

chapter four

zer was having trouble with the wooden bucket – and that was *before* it had any water in it. It was too much for a child of his age, but still he was struggling with it like a hero. Ruel watched him tottering down the bank towards the mill and the river, and it made him feel sick. It was Ruel's job to fetch the water, not Ezer's. It wasn't fair to let his little brother bust his guts over the job like this. But there was nothing Ruel could do about it. He was grounded. His parents had said they wouldn't let him out to do even the quickest of jobs if it meant going out of their sight. He was watching Ezer now from the shadows of their cottage doorway, which was as near to freedom as they'd let him get.

He hadn't found Baladan when he'd charged after him into the trees yesterday morning. He'd only been a few minutes behind the man but there wasn't a sign of him. He'd even shouted – not a clever thing to do in the forest – you never knew who or what you might attract – but there was no reply. When he *did* finally run into someone, just before noon, it wasn't Baladan he met but his father Maaz with half a dozen men from the village. They'd been searching since late the previous afternoon, when they'd realised Ruel was missing, and they were exhausted. They were also very angry – the way grown-ups are when they're relieved after a big fright – so it had seemed like a good idea not to tell them about the meeting with Baladan in case it frightened them even more. He'd kept quiet, let them shout all they wanted, and been brought back to Hazar late last night in disgrace.

Ruel couldn't bear to watch his little brother any longer.

He went back into the cottage and closed the door on the world. He threw himself onto his bed so hard he made clouds of dust rise into the shaft of sunlight that came through the hole in the roof. He was furious with himself. A fine big brother he'd turned out to be – dashing off into the forest on his quest to save them all. He'd achieved nothing – except to make a fool of himself, scare his parents, and land Ezer with a pile of extra work.

He closed his eyes and went off into all kinds of angry daydreams. Most of all he found himself blaming Baladan for disappearing on purpose – how else could a man and a horse have vanished that fast? He was just in the middle of an imaginary argument with Baladan about it, when the cottage door crashed against the wall, and Ezer's stocky little body stood framed in the gap. He had no bucket, and he was panting.

'Where's Dad?' he called out, urgently.

Ruel didn't have time to answer before the big outline of Maaz appeared in the doorway. He had been working in the fields behind the cottages and must have seen his son tearing back home.

'What's the matter?' he asked.

Ezer pointed away up the track in the direction of Kiriath.

'There's someone in the trees,' he whispered.

Maaz stepped into the shadow of the cottage for a moment to pick up his quarterstaff – a pole as tall as himself, the standard weapon in Hazar – then he took up position a couple of metres from the doorway, staff braced across his body, ready for anything.

'I just saw him, standing in the trees,' Ezer explained to Ruel. 'He wasn't moving or anything. It's spooky.'

They both watched their father's broad back, blocking out most of the light. After a while, they saw Maaz relax and rest the butt of his quarterstaff on the ground. Their mother

Naama appeared from behind the cottage and stood beside her husband for a moment. They mumbled a few words that the boys couldn't hear and Maaz handed his wife the staff, ambling away, back to his work.

Naama came into the cottage and propped the staff in its place.

'It's all right,' she said. 'It's just a poor beggar man – your father says he won't do us any harm.'

'What does he want?' Ezer asked.

'Something to eat, I suppose.'

'Are we going to give him something?'

Naama knelt down beside her son and put her hand on his shoulder.

'Darling, we haven't *got* anything,' she said.

'Maybe someone else has.'

'I don't think so, my love.'

'What about Machir? He must have something to spare.'

Naama straightened up a bit stiffly.

'Yes,' she said, in a sharp little voice they didn't hear very often from their mother, 'and he got it by not giving anything away.'

She took Ezer by the shoulders and steered him towards the door.

'Come on, love,' she said. 'I need that water.'

When he'd gone, she asked Ruel if he wanted anything, but he didn't reply. His face was set hard and he wouldn't look at her. She stood beside her son for a moment as if she wanted to say something else, but nothing came. At last she left him and went back outside.

❦

Ezer was nervous, even though Maaz had said there was no danger. Before he set off to pick up the big bucket from where he'd dropped it, he looked around to see if he could see the strange beggar man. He thought he'd probably be heading straight out of the village if there was no food on offer, and he was right. He spotted him down by Zilla's, where the path disappeared into the trees. That was all right, then. Ezer was just about to go on with his job when he saw something that stopped him again. Zilla came out and started to chat to the man; and after a moment she actually took him inside her hovel. Was *she* going to feed him? Everyone said Zilla ate mashed up frogs – was she going to give some of *them* to the man? Since Ruel had told him about Hanan, Ezer had started to be very curious about Zilla. He decided to find out what she was up to.

He knew Naama wanted the water quickly, but it would only take a minute to check on Zilla. He pelted full speed to the end of the village and when he was a few metres from her hovel, he threw himself into the long grass beside the path. He could see her door was open, and he crept up carefully until he could just peep round the frame. She had a fire going and the man was squatting by it, scraping away at something in a bowl. Ezer screwed his eyes up to get a good look but he was disappointed – it looked more like porridge than mashed frogs. Then something amazing happened – much more amazing than eating frogs. The man finished his food, put down the bowl and undid a purse hanging from his belt. He brought out a coin and handed it over to Zilla. As he held it out, it caught the light of the fire and Ezer saw that it was gold.

He was so astonished that he forgot that he was supposed to be hiding, and when the man suddenly turned to look at the door he didn't move – not even when the man met his eyes, got up and came towards him. Ezer knew he was going to get a clout round the ear at best and still he didn't seem able to move a muscle. But the miracles weren't over yet –

instead of taking a swipe at him, the man just held out another gold coin. *Now* Ezer moved – like lightning. He snatched the coin before the man could blink and was heading for home with it as fast as he could run.

~~~

'Ruel, look!' he shouted. 'Look what he gave me!'

Ezer had come crashing through the cottage door, and now he was thrusting something under his brother's nose. Ruel stared. He knew straight away what it was, although he'd never seen one in his life before; but he couldn't work out what on earth it was doing in their cottage, and certainly not what it was doing in Ezer's grubby little hand. It was a gold coin. Even in the dimness of the cottage it glowed; and it made you feel warm just to look at it.

Ezer had started shouting for his family when he was half way down the street, and seconds later, Maaz and Naama appeared.

'Bring it here,' their father ordered.

He took the coin from Ezer and went to the door to get a proper look. He tried to hold it lightly but his big hands were made for gripping tools, not messing around with tiny scraps like this and he dropped it. Ezer pounced like a cat before it could roll, and gave it back. Maaz laid it on the palm of his hand and held it to the sun. He seemed almost frightened of it.

'What did you say, son?' he asked. 'Did you say someone *gave* it to you?'

Ezer let fly with the whole story and seemed to get through it in one breath.

When he'd finished, Maaz stared at the coin a moment longer then gave it to Naama and wandered out into the light like someone sleepwalking. Naama hid the coin and followed her husband outside without a word.

'What do you think it's worth?' Ezer asked his brother.

'Dunno,' he said, 'half a year's wages maybe – half a year's wages for a real top craftsman.'

'Like they have in Kiriath?'

'Yeah – a stone mason, something like that.'

'And all for a bowl of – whatever it was.'

Ruel was staring at the rectangle of light that was their doorway, but his mind was somewhere else, and a crazy suspicion was growing in him.

'What's this man like?' he asked.

'Really rough – cracked old leather clothes. Tall. Thin. Long, straggly black hair. Nothing special. Except for his eyes – he's got weird eyes – sort of fierce and friendly at the same time – not scary.'

'Has he got a horse?'

Ezer laughed. 'You're joking!' he said. 'How would a man like that have a horse?'

'How would he have a purse with gold coins in it?' Ruel asked.

As they were talking they both realised there was something going on outside – people were on the move – there was a lot of excited chatter and it was getting louder. They could hear Machir the miller's voice shouting to people to get out of his way, and other people shouting back. Ezer scrambled up and made for the door, and Ruel followed him. Ezer was off like a shot into the crowd, but Ruel just stood in the doorway and stared. He'd never seen anything like it. People were running down the street towards their homes, some of them – even grown-ups – were skipping and dancing, and waving gold coins in the air. Down by the mill was a crowd of people who hadn't got a coin yet, and in the middle of them, giving out the gold was the man. Ruel found that he wasn't surprised to see it was Baladan.

When they'd met in the forest, Ruel hadn't realised how tall Baladan was, but now, amongst the villagers, Ruel could see that he towered above them all. Casually Baladan raised his head to look up the bank towards Ruel's cottage, almost as if he knew where to look and what to expect, and their eyes met over the heads of the crowd. It was only a moment, not long enough for anyone else to notice, but long enough for Ruel to feel a surge of excitement and a ridiculous sense that somehow everything would be all right now; but before that feeling could take proper hold, there came a blast of anger – anger that Baladan had abandoned him in the forest, had made him look stupid, had let him down in some way. The anger blew everything else away, and Ruel swung round, plunging back into the cottage and banging the door behind him.

<hr>

After Baladan had finished giving the gold coins out and every household in the village had got one, there was a strange quiet about the place. The truth was, the villagers hadn't got a clue what to *do* with the money. It took until the next morning for someone to have an idea. It was Machir the miller who showed them the way. He was the only one in the village who'd ever seen a gold coin before. Maybe he'd even held one once. Some people made out that he had a sack of them buried under the mill, but that couldn't be right because he'd stared at his coin as stupidly as anyone else when he'd elbowed his way through the crush and grabbed it. Halak the blacksmith said he'd been drooling over it like a dog, but Maaz reckoned that was an exaggeration.

Whether he'd drooled or not, he was certainly eager to be doing something with his treasure. He was up before the birds the next morning, and on his way along the eastern track to Kiriath. He'd left his apprentice, Chilion, in charge of the mill with strict instructions not to tell anyone where he'd gone. But Chilion, being Chilion, the whole village knew by sunrise – it wasn't often that a young man had such a piece of news to feel important about. What Chilion *didn't* know, because he hadn't been told, was what Machir had gone to Kiriath to do. The village was wild with rumours and guesses.

It was three days before they found out. Then they thought he'd bought himself an army with his gold – that's what it sounded like, coming down the track. They could hear the rumbling half a kilometre away. But when Machir finally appeared, sweating, red in the face, and shouting instructions, it wasn't a siege engine that followed him out of the trees, but a wagon. Machir and the three men he'd brought with him looked exhausted – it must have been a nightmare trying to get a thing like that down the forest track. But exhausted or not, he didn't give himself or the men a minute to rest – they started unloading straight away. And what they unloaded were tools and materials to build a house – a proper house – the kind you find in town – the kind you would find in Kiriath.

By nightfall Machir's 'estate' – the open ground beside his mill – had been cleared, levelled and marked out, and the first post-holes dug. Jarib had been with one or two of the more argumentative characters in Hazar to complain that the ground was the village meeting place and didn't belong to Machir – but the miller got Chilion and his three workmen lined up behind him with axes in their hands and told Jarib to prove it or clear off. There was no proof of anything to do with owning things in Hazar, seeing there was so little to own. The only decisions on things like that were made by the village assembly, and Jarib seemed to think the village didn't want to meet just then.

He was right. The village wasn't bothered about stopping Machir, they were too interested in copying him. Next day a whole party set off for Kiriath. And in the days that followed, every single cottage in Hazar, except for Zilla's and Jarib's, sent someone down the eastern track to town. There followed a trail of wagons back to Hazar, and soon the way had been made so wide that it wasn't a struggle for them any more. Back and forward the wagons went, bringing stone, tiles, all the stuff for plaster, even some glass for real windows – and always more labourers. Talking to them, it sounded as if the whole area for miles around Kiriath had been stripped of every available builder. Apparently, there were even wild rumours in the town that someone was building a great castle in the forest, and a sergeant with half a dozen scruffy soldiers turned up to check on what was happening.

They went back to Kiriath with news of the strange man and his purse of gold, and soon a rather smarter squad of soldiers with an officer in charge arrived with a message to say that Baron Azal would like to meet the 'gold-giver'. The soldiers found Baladan hard at work helping pull down the cottage that belonged to Chilion's mother. Unlike Machir, no one else in Hazar had any spare ground near them, so everyone was having to destroy their mud cottage before they could start to build a proper house. Baladan had volunteered his services wherever they were needed and had amazed everyone by the strength in his wiry body, and the skill in his hands.

He amazed them, too, by the way he dealt with the soldiers. It was pretty unusual to see one of Azal's officers in a forest village, but when you did, you kept your eyes down when you talked to him, and you did whatever you were told. So a shiver went through the crowd that had gathered round when Baladan straightened up from his work and looked this officer straight in the eye. Being so tall, he had to look down his nose to do it, and the officer had to look up – obviously not something he was used to. He wasn't used to the kind of reply he got to his message either.

'Tell Baron Azal that I *will* come to see him,' Baladan said, 'but not just yet – the time isn't right.'

The officer just stared back with his mouth open, looking foolish. Everyone expected swords to come out, or at least some serious shouting, but instead the officer suddenly ordered an about-turn, mounted up and led his men back the way they'd come. The villagers stared down the track after them, but Baladan simply got on with what he'd been doing as if nothing had happened.

With the excitement over, everyone went back to their work; everyone except Ruel. His parents had allowed him out again after a few days and he had bumped into Baladan several times in the fortnight he'd now been in Hazar. But they had never gone beyond a nod to acknowledge that they knew each other. It felt like a kind of stubbornness on Ruel's part. The anger he'd felt at first had settled into a sour resentment. But the truth was, he also felt embarrassed. The business of his 'quest' seemed stupid now, and Baladan knew more about it than anyone. Ruel actually wanted to forget about the whole thing. The only trouble was that he couldn't forget – because he couldn't forget about Safir. He'd joined in with all the new activity in Hazar, and tried io get excited about it, but deep inside there was always the pain of his lost sister. He desperately needed to talk. And he still desperately wanted to *do* something.

It was seeing Baladan face the soldiers that broke Ruel's silence. As he watched Baladan send the officer away with his tail between his legs, hope flared up again inside him. Ruel waited until Baladan was on his own, then he went and stood beside him. Baladan put down his tools and looked at Ruel. Every time they'd come across each other, Ruel had felt that if they were going to talk, he'd have to be the first to speak, and it was the same now. He took a deep breath.

'Why did you leave me?' he asked.

It was a foolish question. Ruel knew that Baladan could simply say, 'Why didn't you follow me when you had the chance?' And as he waited for him to say it, Ruel suddenly knew that all his anger against Baladan was really anger with himself for having been too slow. But Baladan didn't say it. He just smiled. And it wasn't the kind of smile that makes fun of you. It was the kind of smile you get from a friend.

'I'm here now, aren't I?' he said, and he put his hand on Ruel's shoulder.

Now that the ice was broken, Ruel didn't know what to say, except the one thing that was filling his heart.

'I can't stop thinking about Safir,' he blurted out. 'I've got to do something. You've got to help me.'

Slowly, Baladan bowed his head.

What did *that* mean? Was he nodding agreement, or just saying he understood?

'Be patient,' Baladan told him. 'The time will come.'

Then there was silence, and Ruel could tell he was going to get nothing more out of Baladan on that subject. But now he'd started he wasn't going to let the moment pass without saying something else that was on his mind. Everyone knew that since that first day in Hazar, Baladan had spent a lot of time down at the hovel where the path met the woods.

'How's Zilla?' Ruel asked.

'She's fine,' Baladan told him. 'She talks about you a lot. She misses you.'

As he thought about his old friend, Ruel realised how lonely his life had become and how much he needed a friend.

'I'm glad you spoke to me,' Baladan said. 'I've been waiting.'

It wasn't long after that, that Ruel and Ezer found out exactly what their gold coin was worth – enough to finish half a house. Maaz and the men he had hired had got the walls well established; Baladan had come to help for a couple of days and had taught Ruel and Ezer how to mix plaster and put it on so it didn't fall off again; then the end of the month arrived, and the men asked to be paid up to date. Maaz went to Naama for the gold coin, handed it over and waited for some change. He didn't get any. They told him the coin didn't quite cover the work they'd done so far. It was the same story all over Hazar. Panic set in as one after another the builders found their employer's money had run out and started to pack their things up ready to leave.

But Baladan came to the rescue. Quietly he went round to every half-built house and slipped another gold coin into each owner's hand, saying, 'If you need any more, just come and ask.'

Money flowed again; the builders unslung their leather bags from their shoulders, and the work went on. After that, people started to wonder how many gold coins were *in* the stranger's purse. Although he ate with Zilla, Baladan slept out amongst the trees and Chilion – always the one to be first with the news – claimed he'd crept out to spy on Baladan and seen a great war horse out there where he was camped with lots of saddlebags and things unloaded on the ground. It didn't take long before everyone in Hazar was convinced that each one of those bags was stuffed with gold.

On the strength of this, the place went quietly mad. The villagers started spending as if money really was growing on the trees all around them. Their plans got more and more grand – the half-built houses were pulled down and started again on bigger foundations; single storey buildings were strengthened to take a second storey; wall hangings and carved furniture were ordered from Kiriath. Halak the blacksmith worked from first light of dawn, and his furnace roared long into the night. He laughed and sang as he worked, whilst Machir the miller spluttered and choked with joy in the dust clouds inside his mill. The two of them were the only people in Hazar who seemed to be earning as much as they spent as they turned out flour and nails for the workmen by the sackful. And all the time, the only thing anyone needed to do to get hold of another glowing coin was to have a quiet word with Baladan.

So the weeks passed. Sometimes, Baladan would come to help with Ruel's house and take the time to teach the boy some new skill. Always Ruel would ask how long it would be before they could do something about Safir, but always the answer was the same: 'Patience'. Baladan seemed to be able to do anything he turned his hand to, and it was hard for Ruel not to admire him, but it was hard, too, not to lose his temper with that word: patience was something Ruel had never had much of. But Baladan seemed to be his only hope, and so Ruel found that he was always glad to see him. He was also glad of the news Baladan would bring of Zilla. Talking about her with Baladan made it feel as if he was still seeing her; and when he said this to Baladan one day, he told him that Zilla had said exactly the same.

Spring edged slowly towards summer. The evenings were getting longer. And it was during one of these long, warm evenings, when all the smells of the fields and the forest and the animals mix into a beautiful perfume like the scent of someone you love, that a terrible rumour began to spread round Hazar. Apparently one of the villagers had been to ask Baladan for more gold, as normal, and he'd been told that there *was* no more. A group of villagers went to demand an explanation from Baladan, but they couldn't find him.

Chilion took some men to where he said Baladan had been camped, but there was no sign of him there either. The village went crazy – it was ten times worse than when the first coins had run out: not only were there buildings without roofs all over Hazar but now, away in Kiriath, there were pieces of furniture and clothing and decorations half carved or woven and no payments made on them. Nothing was completely finished, nothing was completely paid for. At once the builders started looking round to see what they could strip and sell to recover their losses. The dreams of Hazar had turned into a nightmare.

chapter five

Groups of angry, panicky people were wandering aimlessly in the street and in between the cottages. It was evening. The daylight was going and so was any hope of finding Baladan. Then suddenly a great shout shook the air, echoing all over the village.

'He's by the river!' It was Halak, who had lungs the size of his bellows.

There was a rush down to the open space in front of the big rocks. Some of the men had their quarterstaffs – although what good they thought those were going to be, it was hard to say. Maybe they thought they could *beat* more gold out of Baladan.

When Ruel and his family got down to the river, they saw the unmistakable outline of Baladan standing on the biggest rock. He was absolutely still, and his stillness seemed to bring everyone to order. All the muttering died away in front of him and the crowd stood silent. Ruel stared at him hard. This was the man who kept saying that there would come a time to go after Safir. Ruel didn't care much about finishing the buildings in Hazar, but he cared a lot about whether Baladan could be trusted.

'You're worried about the gold,' Baladan said, at last. 'Don't be.'

There was an uncertain murmur.

'Didn't you *ever* wonder where the gold *came* from?' Baladan went on.

'Who cares, as long as it's there!' someone shouted – it sounded like Chilion.

'Well – it's time you knew – you *need* to know.'

Baladan let them wait and wonder a moment longer before he told them.

'It's The Dragon's gold,' he said.

There was dead silence, as if the heart of the village had stopped. Then there was a single wail from one of the women – a long wail – as long as her breath lasted.

'You've stolen from The Dragon,' an old man shouted. 'It'll kill us all!'

'I've stolen nothing,' Baladan replied. 'I've only taken back what The Dragon has stolen from *you* over many years. That was no more than simple justice. But now it's time to deal with The Dragon so that it can never steal from you again. I've come here to kill it – but I can't do that alone. I need help – *your* help.'

He pointed behind them, to the jagged tooth of the mountain rising beyond the trees – a black shape against the darkening sky. Apart from the river, it was the only landmark in their lives. They turned to look at it, and a shiver ran through the crowd. It was an evil place – a place that none of them had ever been to.

'That's where we'll meet The Dragon,' Baladan told them. 'Up on the top of that mountain is its lair. And in its lair is more gold. When we've dealt with The Dragon, the gold will be yours for the taking.'

'Let's take it then!' cried a young hothead called Zethar.

One or two muttered in agreement, but most people were too shocked to think what should be done.

'What do you say?' Baladan asked the crowd. 'Who's with me?'

There wasn't a clear response, and soon the villagers turned away from Baladan into little groups, everyone talking eagerly to their neighbours, or talking at them, more like – everyone jabbering, and no one listening. Maaz was almost shouting in the face of the man next to him and the man's wife was babbling at Naama.

'What's the point of living in a big house?' Naama shouted back at the woman. 'I never wanted it anyway. It won't bring Safir back.'

'Why are you still moping about her? Forget her – she's dead,' the woman snapped at her, impatiently.

Ruel's head had been whirling with everything that was going on, but this suddenly brought him up short. 'No she's not!' he shouted.

The woman laughed. 'Your boy's mad, Naama,' she said.

Naama moved away sharply, pulling Ezer behind her.

Ruel wormed his way to the edge of the crowd and sat down. He felt shocked. It wasn't what the woman had said so much as the *way* she'd said it. He thought back to the time when Safir had first been taken. No one would have spoken about her like that then – or about him. No one had called him mad for running off into the forest. A strange hardness had crept into people's hearts these last weeks whilst they'd been so busy building and planning. This wasn't the old Hazar; he hadn't really noticed it before, but Ruel suddenly saw it now, and he didn't like it. He realised that if Safir returned, it wouldn't just be the houses she wouldn't recognise any more.

He was still sitting by himself, thinking, when Ezer came to find him a few minutes later.

'Why did you say that about Safir?' he asked.

'I don't know,' Ruel replied.

'She *is* dead though, isn't she?'

Ruel stared at the grass between his feet. It was just about dark now and he had to screw up his eyes to make out the pattern of the blades.

'I feel as if *I've* been dead inside ever since she went,' he said, 'but what that woman said brought something to life again.'

'What do you mean?'

'You know the way I could always tell where she was?'

'So *you* said!'

'I could! And I can tell it again now – the feeling's come back inside me.'

'Go on then – where is she?'

'It's not like that this time – I can't tell where she *is* exactly, I just know she's *somewhere*.' Ruel took his brother by the shoulders as if he really needed to make him understand. 'Can you think how you'd feel if you suddenly saw Safir again,' he went on, 'what it'd feel like inside – how your heart'd jump? That's how I felt just now. It's as if Safir had to do something desperate when the woman said she was dead – like she shouted out from a long way away to make us believe she's still alive. Well, it worked. I know it now. I *know* she's not dead.'

Ezer felt that he agreed with the woman – his brother was mad. And he might have said so too, if his mother hadn't turned up just then.

'We're going home,' she told them.

'What's happening?' Ruel asked.

'Jarib says we need to sleep before we decide what to do – we're going to meet again at daybreak.'

Next morning lookouts were sent far into the forest to watch for any danger from The Dragon. Why on earth people should think they had to do that now was beyond reason. They'd been living off The Dragon's gold unknowingly for weeks and it hadn't attacked them. But now they knew whose money had been paying for their new village there was a panicky feeling that the revenge of The Dragon might fall on their heads at any minute. There was no point in fighting, but if they got warning, at least they could run.

Whilst the lookouts stood guard, the village assembly got started. They had to go down by the rocks, now that Machir's 'estate' was built on. Jarib asked Baladan to sit next to him, which he did, but he said right at the start that he wasn't going to speak – he'd said all he had to say the night before. He would just listen and wait for them to decide what they wanted to do. Jarib accepted that, set the question before the assembly – to go with Baladan to face The Dragon or not – and sat down to let the talking start.

Maaz was the first to speak. When he stood up, everyone seemed to straighten their backs and pay attention. His fiery temper had always made people take notice of him, but since losing Safir there seemed to be a new weight about him as if the sadness had planted his feet more firmly on the ground, and now people tended to listen to him with extra respect.

'We want gold,' he said. 'We *need* gold. That's our fault. What Baladan gave us was a repayment of what was owed us – what we chose to *do* with the money was our own responsibility, and some of us might be thinking now that our choices were foolish. But we can't get away from the consequences – we need gold to finish what we've started. But gold isn't what *Baladan* wants. He wants to kill The Dragon. We mustn't let ourselves be blinded to that by the hope of more gold. If we want to get what *we* want, we're going to have to do what *Baladan* wants. We mustn't forget that.'

Maaz sat down, and straight away Chilion was on his feet. He was starting to make quite a name for himself these days, too, but although he always had something to say, people were not usually too keen to hear it. People didn't shout each other down at these meetings – that wasn't the way they did things – but they showed by the way they shuffled about that they wished Chilion would shut up.

'Maaz is right,' he said. 'This is all about fighting The Dragon. And in that case there's no argument – we've been through this before a hundred times – it can't be done. There's no point in even thinking about it. No one's ever won against The Dragon before and they're not going to do it now. Baladan might have got lucky and managed to sneak a few bags of gold away from The Dragon – but, I ask you, is a sneak thief going to be able to kill a dragon? I mean, look at him – he's got arms like twigs compared to a real man like Halak, and even Halak wouldn't try and stand up to The Dragon. Anyway, how do we know all that gold came from The Dragon in the first place? Maybe Baladan just stole it from a castle somewhere – maybe he stole it from Baron Azal – maybe that's why they came looking for him that time. Maybe that's why he's been so keen to give it away – to get rid of it, because he's scared. I think this is all a con.'

Chilion seemed to run out of wind. He stood there for a moment as if he was waiting for another idea to come into his head, then he gave up and sat down again. He was slightly red in the face. Everyone looked at Baladan, to see how he would take the comments that had been made, but he was just poking at something in the grass with a stick and didn't seem to be taking any notice. The question of why he'd given them all the gold in the first place had startled many of them and it weighed on their minds. It was a new thought. Whilst things were going well, it simply hadn't occurred to them to be suspicious, but now they couldn't help wondering if he'd been leading them into some sort of trap. Because trapped was certainly how they felt.

There was an embarrassing pause, then it was Zilla that got up to speak. A little breeze took hold of her white hair and shook it with its coloured ribbons, and her rough, rainbow gown filled out like the sail of a ship. The fact that she'd stayed in her hovel and not got involved in all the building in the village these last weeks seemed to make her more mad than ever to many of the villagers. But there were a few who'd taken notice of the fact that Baladan ate with her, and that the only other person who'd not torn down their old cottage was Jarib – the wisest man any of them had ever known. These people were starting to put two and two together and have a rather different opinion of Zilla.

'Chilion is right,' she said. 'We *have* been through this all before – when he was a little baby, and not the fine grown man he is now.'

There was a welcome ripple of laughter, and Chilion shuffled uncomfortably.

'It's obvious that this is about standing up to The Dragon. It's a pity that it's taken greed to get you to think about it again, but that's what this is all about – there's no getting away from it. There was a man once who disagreed with you, Chilion – a man who said it *could* be done. That man was called Hanan.'

Ruel's heart was thumping. He expected Zilla to go on and tell the tale of Hanan again. But she didn't. She just stood there with the breeze billowing her gown, and let the name hang in the air. No one was supposed to speak whilst someone else was on their feet and so there was a long silence before at last she sat down.

It was Chilion's mother who got up next.

'Hanan never told us *how* it could be done,' was all she said.

Naama got up, 'He said the King would come,' she reminded them.

Then it was Halak who stood. A murmur ran round the gathering – no one could remember the last time the blacksmith had had anything to say at an assembly. But people sitting near to him weren't surprised. He seemed to have been shifting around and stirring himself to get up ever since Chilion had mentioned his name.

'The King didn't come,' Halak said, 'but maybe he *will* if we make a move. Maybe he was waiting for us to have the guts to do something. Maybe he's still waiting.' He stopped for a moment and took a big breath. 'If you decide to go after The Dragon,' he said, 'you can count me in.'

That really set people going. Up until then it had all been hot air, but if Halak said he would go with Baladan, that made it seem possible that they might actually give it a try. A lot of people got up to speak and they were all looking pale and their voices were shaky. Everyone knew this was serious now and that they might actually have to make a decision to go or not to go. They knew straight away that if they decided to stay they'd feel bad, and if they went they'd probably die. It was a no-win situation – unless they killed The Dragon. And everyone in their hearts agreed with Chilion on that – deep down no one had the slightest doubt that it was impossible. Halak had got them to the edge of a cliff and they were desperate to escape, but no one dared be the one to suggest they turn around.

That was the moment when one of the builders from Kiriath got up. He turned to Jarib. 'You've invited us to sit with you this morning, sir,' he said, 'but you haven't told us if we can speak.'

Jarib rose. 'If you eat and sleep and work in Hazar, you live in Hazar,' he said, 'and if you live in Hazar you are part of the assembly – say what you have to say.'

The man looked round at the other builders. 'I think I can speak for the rest of us who've come from Kiriath and thereabouts,' he said, 'and I have to say I'm finding all this worrying about The Dragon very strange. We don't have that in Kiriath at all. I can't remember the last time anyone had anything to say about dragons. We've lived in peace for years – Baron Azal protects us. Instead of going out to fight this dragon, why don't you just go up to Kiriath and ask Baron Azal to take your village under his protection? He's kept Kiriath and all the villages round about free from dragons all this time – I'm sure he can do it for this place too.'

It was as if the sun had come out. People seemed to stretch and smile all around, but Ruel felt empty. There was something wrong. It seemed too easy. Then he realised two things – Zilla was standing again, and Baladan had looked up.

'This is King's Land,' Zilla said, in a voice that seemed suddenly as big as Halak's, 'ancient King's Land – King's Land from the beginning of our history. It's not ours to be giving away to Azal or anyone. How can we ask Baron Azal to protect us? The *King* protects us and no one else.'

There were no dramatic pauses this time. She sat down with a bump, looking completely shocked at what had been suggested. There were one or two murmurs of agreement with what she'd said from the older folk, but all in all there didn't seem to be too many other people who felt the same way.

Machir got up with a nasty smirk on his face.

'The King protects us,' he said with a sneer. 'Exactly! These last few weeks are the first good times any of us can remember in a lifetime of being 'protected' by the King – and did the King give the good times to us? Not a bit of it! A thief had to show us the way.' He bowed respectfully to Baladan.

'It takes one to know one!' someone muttered, loud enough for everyone to hear. There was laughter – relief was catching hold of the assembly. Machir scowled around him, until everyone was quiet again.

'I'll tell you what I *do* know, friend,' he said, with a real bite in his voice. 'I know that that thief in his cracked leather exists – which is more than I can say about the mad woman's "King". Quit while you're ahead is my motto. Baladan has taken back what The Dragon owes us for years of terror, and if Baron Azal can protect us from any retaliation, I say let's run to him with open arms.'

'You *would* say that,' said Maaz, jumping up the moment the miller was back on his haunches. 'Quit while you're ahead? You're ahead and no mistake – you've made a packet out of selling to the builders!'

It wasn't clear whether Maaz had anything else to say, because he was cut off by a sudden shout up on the village street. Everyone turned to see one of the lookouts charging down the bank towards them. People jumped up, fearing the worst.

It was Zethar – always the first to volunteer for anything, he'd led the lookouts that morning. He barged through the crowd and scrambled up the rocks where they could all see him. He was something of a sight, too – thick, shoulder-length, dark hair flying in the breeze, brown eyes flashing, clothes torn from his sprint through the trees, chest bare to the belly shining with sweat and heaving. All of a sudden he seemed to realise that he hadn't got any breath left to speak with and bent double with his hands on his knees, gasping. There was another shout from the treeline, as two more lookouts made for the crowd. Zethar straightened up quickly, throwing his hair back, and made sure he spoke first.

'Reaper,' he said, 'three of us saw him – didn't come near us – don't know if he saw us – definitely him – no mistake.'

Zethar was Chilion's friend, and Chilion now leaped up beside him on the rock.

'It's The Dragon's revenge!' he shouted. 'The Dragon wants another sacrifice to make up for its treasure!'

There didn't seem to be any doubt about it. Losing Safir was recent history as far as giving sacrifices went. The Dragon expected crops and animals regularly, but it only sent the Reaper for a victim once a year. This was much too soon after Safir for an ordinary sacrifice to be demanded.

'Aye,' a man shouted in the crowd, 'and we know who to send!'

Straight away half a dozen men grabbed hold of Baladan and started dragging him towards the trees. No one tried to stop them, and most people were shouting in agreement. Ruel was shocked and horrified. The villagers had suddenly become a mob and for the first time in his life, he didn't feel safe amongst them. He looked round desperately for his father, and saw Maaz staring at the group of men heading for the trees. He wasn't shouting, but he wasn't doing anything to stop them, either.

Then two surprising things happened almost at once. Halak charged up the hill like a bull and blocked the men's way; and the moment they stopped, somehow Baladan got himself free from them. They seemed too astonished by how he'd done it to make a move, and he took a few steps away from them, then turned to face the villagers, strung out now all the way down the bank to the river. When he spoke, he didn't seem to shout, but his voice carried right to the back of the crowd.

'You don't need to drag me,' he said, 'I'll go myself to see this Reaper. If The Dragon wants a sacrifice, we'll see what it makes of me – with your help, it'll find it's bitten off more than it can chew. Is anyone coming with me?'

He stared at the crowd, and there was a pause. Then one by one, and without a sound, they began to melt away from those powerful eyes. Almost the first to go were the men who'd dragged him towards the woods. Machir probably beat them by half a minute – his mill door slamming was the first sound to break the silence. Soon most of the villagers had not only left the gathering, but had followed Machir's example and shut their doors. Amongst the last to go was Zethar, still perched on the rock. Chilion was pulling at him and hissing for him to come away but he seemed riveted by Baladan's eyes. It was only with a great effort that Chilion got him home. The last of all to leave was Halak. His shoulders seemed to droop as he watched more and more of the villagers disappear, and when he saw there was nobody left but him, he bowed his head and slunk away himself, looking half his normal size.

Though the doors were shut, there were some faces peeking round the edges of their newly installed window frames. They saw Baladan wait a moment on his own, then whistle softly. For the first time, they saw the great war horse they'd heard so many rumours about and which seemed to disappear and appear again as mysteriously as Baladan himself. It trotted easily out of the trees and came up to its master. In a single movement Baladan was on its back. And quietly, horse and rider melted away into the trees. He may have left the new Hazar half finished, but in their hearts none of those peeping from their windows felt sorry to see him go.

chapter six

Baladan only went a little way into the shadow of the trees. He brought his horse to a standstill where he could still hear the creak of Machir's mill – and waited. He stayed completely still in the saddle, gazing ahead through the dark crowd of tree trunks. His horse swished its tail gently from time to time. This was the only movement. Whatever they were waiting for, it looked as if the horse and its rider were ready to wait there for ever.

It was actually less than five minutes before a crunch of twigs made the horse swing its head. A moment or two more, then Baladan himself turned to smile at the person who pushed her way through the undergrowth and came huffing and puffing up to his stirrup. It was Zilla.

'I'm sorry everyone deserted you,' she said.

'Everyone except you,' he pointed out.

She looked down at the mossy ground, embarrassed. 'I know,' she said, 'but what use am I against a dragon?'

'I'd rather have you than an army,' Baladan told her. 'There's more power in your eyes than any dragon in the world could stand up to.'

She looked him in the face and smiled. 'Really?' she said. 'Do you mean it?'

He swung down from his horse and handed the reins to her.

'Can you ride?' he asked.

Zilla wasn't often stuck for something to say, but she was just then. She looked at Baladan and then at the horse, then back at Baladan again.

'I don't know,' she said, at last. 'I've never tried.'

'Meet Hesed.' He patted the horse's neck. 'He'll teach you.'

'But he's huge!'

'Not half as big as a dragon – come on, up you go!'

And with some rather undignified heaving, Zilla ended up in a side-saddle position on Hesed's back.

'Comfortable?' Baladan asked.

'Yes, it's not bad at all. But I don't know what I'm going to do if he moves.'

'Well, he won't for a bit – there's someone else we have to pick up before we set off. You just make friends with old Hesed whilst we wait.'

So Zilla chatted softly to Hesed, and the great horse cocked his ears, for all the world as if he was listening – even sighing from time to time to keep the conversation up. And Baladan leaned against a tree trunk, gently playing with a leaf and looking way up above him from time to time to catch the twinkle of sunlight coming through the holes in the roof of the forest.

A few moments later, a rustle told them someone else was coming and Baladan straightened up to meet the new arrival.

'You nearly let me get away again,' he said to Ruel.

'Hello, dearie – look at me,' said Zilla, beaming from her perch. But then her smile died and she started struggling as if she was trying to get off Hesed's back.

'Look out,' said Baladan, 'you'll break a leg if you fall from up there.'

'I think I'd better get down and go back,' she said sadly.

Ruel knew why at once. Coming suddenly face-to-face with her like this, after all the weeks of being apart, had given him that shocked feeling you get when you know you're doing something you shouldn't. His parents' ban on seeing Zilla still stood. Baladan knew the problem too –

separately, they'd both told him all about it. Now they found themselves looking at him for guidance, as if it was the natural thing to do.

'I see what you mean,' he said. 'This needs thinking about.' He was silent and closed his eyes for a moment. 'Parents make the rules for a family,' he said at last, 'and that's important. But who makes the rules for the parents?'

Ruel looked puzzled, But Zilla seemed to get what he was driving at.

'The King,' she said.

'Correct – and what do you think the King wants to happen about The Dragon?'

'He wants it killed – Hanan came to tell us that,' Zilla answered.

'Right again,' Baladan went on, 'and I'm here to do it. But I've told you, I need help. What I *didn't* say in the village is that I need *your* help. If you don't come with me – both of you – it can't be done. If either of you goes back, you'll be doing what Maaz and Naama want, but not what the King wants.'

There was a long silence. Zilla and Ruel didn't look at each other or at Baladan. There was clearly a decision to be made, but it didn't seem as if Baladan wanted to hurry them.

'By the way,' he said to Ruel, after a while, 'do you know what "carrying a lady's favour" means?'

Ruel looked baffled by this change of subject. 'It's something knights do,' he answered. 'Zilla told me about it in a story once. If a knight has a lady's scarf or belt or something wound round some bit of his armour, that's called "carrying her favour" and it means whenever he fights, he's fighting for her.'

'Zilla's a good teacher,' Baladan told him. He jerked his thumb towards the long bundle hanging from Hesed's saddle. 'Have a look in that,' he said.

Ruel went up to the horse and carefully pulled the wrapping from the hilt of the great sword that he knew was in there. As it came away, he suddenly caught his breath. 'What is it, dearie?' asked Zilla.

Ruel held out a strip of pale brown cloth that was tied securely round the top of the scabbard.

'It's Safir's,' he said. 'It's from the hem of her dress. I remember her stitching those flowers on it. She was wearing it the day she was taken.' He swung round to Baladan. 'Where did you get it?'

'Found it in the forest,' he said, 'caught in a bramble.'

Ruel stood for a moment longer, staring at the cloth, his mind whirring.

'Are you saying that because of this, whatever you do, you're doing for Safir?' he asked.

Baladan smiled, in a way Ruel found vaguely annoying. '*You're* saying it now,' he told the boy.

'So, does that mean she's alive?'

Baladan's eyes seemed to search right into Ruel.

'*Is* she alive?' Baladan asked.

He'd spoken softly, but Ruel felt shaken by the force in the question. 'Yes,' he said, rather more weakly than he wanted to. 'Yes, she is.'

There was a pause, and when Baladan spoke again he did so in a brisk businesslike way, as if decisions had been taken. 'Good,' he said. 'I'm glad to hear it. Now, it's time to be going – those who are with me, must come.'

A moment later, Baladan, Ruel, Zilla and Hesed moved off together and melted away into the shadows.

The first place they aimed for was the great fallen tree where Zabad the Reaper would leave the pig's head on a stick that signalled a sacrifice was needed. It was also where he'd come to pick up his victims. But there was no head and no Zabad. They waited around for a while, and made it obvious they were there by shouting out The Reaper's name; but nothing happened, so they pressed on. The middle of the day saw them deep in the forest. Baladan was leading the way.

'Where are we going?' Ruel called to him.

'Where do you think?'

'The mountain?'

There was no reply. Ruel was walking by the horse's head. He looked up at Zilla who was doing better than just staying on Hesed – she was having fun.

'Is this the way to the mountain?' he asked her.

'How should I know?' she said. 'I've never been anywhere near it. Anyway, how am I supposed to know what's the way to anywhere in the middle of this lot? Just enjoy yourself. Baladan knows what he's doing.'

Zilla was certainly enjoying herself. All doubt as to whether she should be with Ruel seemed to have gone.

They had been travelling some time when suddenly Baladan stopped. Without a word being spoken to him, Hesed stopped too. In a moment, Ruel picked up the reason. The training Maaz had given him had taught him to read the sounds of the forest, and he could hear that they were not alone. It was people, not an animal – a small group of people, on the move somewhere away to the left, and they obviously weren't taking care to hide their presence. In fact, after a while it didn't need a forester to tell they were there – you could hear their voices. There seemed to be some arguing, then a sound like a blow landing and a scream.

It was a woman's scream. Baladan picked up the direction of the sound and was off like a shot, slipping left and right round the great tree trunks, and leaping over bushes and brambles like a deer. Hesed might have been big, but he didn't seem to have much trouble weaving after his master – Zilla had to grip the front of the saddle tight and crouch down over the horse's neck to avoid the branches. Ruel brought up the rear as fast as he could. He desperately wanted it to be Safir's voice they'd heard.

All of a sudden, they were out of the thick crowd of trees – out of the shadows into a pale green light. It wasn't a clearing they were in but the pathway cut through the forest by a fast-running stream – one of the many that tumbled down from the mountain to join the river that flowed past Hazar. You could use a stream like this to find your way to the mountain, and it looked as if this was exactly what the group they were chasing was doing. Ruel could see them now, up to his left and on this side of the stream. It was a man and two women. The women were tied up and were being dragged along the bank, stumbling on the stones. The group was about fifty metres away, and Ruel could tell that neither of the women was Safir. Deep down, he'd known.

'Wait!' Baladan shouted.

The man turned round sharply and did as he was told. Baladan told Ruel and Zilla to stay where they were. Ruel expected him to get his sword out and charge, but instead he walked casually and unarmed towards the man and his captives. Baladan stopped when he was a few paces away from the man and the two seemed to look at each other for a while, then Baladan stepped away into the trees. The man tied the end of the rope by which he'd been dragging the women to a thick branch, and followed.

There was a shocked silence between Zilla and Ruel. It was Zilla who broke it.

'That was Zabad,' she said, quietly.

Ruel stared at her as if he didn't understand. 'Are you sure?' he asked.

'I couldn't make a mistake about a thing like that,' she told him. 'I saw him grow up.'

'What?'

'Did no one ever tell you?' she said. 'He's from Hazar.'

Ruel made a decision.

'Come on,' he said, 'we've got to help those women.'

Zilla wasn't sure – they'd been told to stay put, but Ruel insisted and half pulled her off Hesed's back. Together, they set off towards the two prisoners.

The women didn't seem pleased to see them though. As soon as Ruel and Zilla came near, the captives got as far away from them as the rope would let them. Close up, you could see that they were roped together at the waist, their hands were tied behind their backs, and there were even ropes round their ankles so that they couldn't do much more than shuffle along.

'It's all right!' Zilla told them. 'We've come to let you go.'

'Honest – it's all right,' Ruel added, moving slowly forward as if he was dealing with a frightened animal.

'Your friend's gone with The Reaper,' one of the women said. 'We thought you must work for The Reaper.'

Ruel was stunned.

'No, no,' he said. 'Our friend's come to *kill* The Reaper.'

'Then why have they gone off together?' the woman asked.

Ruel didn't have an answer. He and Zilla got to work as best they could on the ropes tying the women up. Ruel had brought the same knife from home that he'd taken last time he ran away, and as soon as he realised he didn't stand a chance of untying the knots, he started hacking through the ropes. They were really tough, and each one took a long time to cut. Whilst he sweated away, Zilla talked to the women, asking them where they'd come from and how Zabad had got hold of them.

It turned out they were from Maon, a little village hidden away in the highlands, east of the mountain. They were sisters. The one who'd spoken to them was called Rizpa. She went on doing most of the talking, her thick coppery hair swinging about as she jutted her chin this way and that. Her face was fierce, and her voice deep and argumentative. She seemed more angry than afraid at the situation they were in. She shouldn't have been with Zabad at all, she told them – it was her sister Lexa who had been chosen as a sacrifice from their village, but Rizpa had refused to be parted from her, so Zabad had taken them both.

Lexa had her sister's strong, definite-looking face, but she seemed much more still and solid. Her hair was short, mousy and she seemed to hold herself back, waiting for the time to speak. When her sister had got her anger out of the way, Lexa told them about Maon. Her voice was lighter than Rizpa's but the kind that made you listen to it. She told them that life in Maon was tough. There were hardly any males there except old men and boys, so the women had to work the land, manage the animals, keep back the trees, take care of the children, and give what protection they could to the village. Two years before, their men had decided they would refuse to give any more sacrifices and would stand up to The Dragon. They'd remembered Hanan and the promise of help from the King and marched off into the forest with quarterstaffs, axes, scythes, anything they could get their hands on for weapons. Not one of them had returned.

Ruel was only half listening to all of this. His hands were working frantically on the ropes, whilst his mind was busy dealing with a lot of doubts and fears – and the little sense he made of what Lexa was saying didn't help make him feel any easier. Everything seemed suddenly hopeless and pointless – but worse than that, their one chance seemed to have turned into part of the danger. What *was* Baladan doing with Zabad? A terrible thought got hold of Ruel and wouldn't let him go. That piece of Safir's dress – had Baladan *really* just found it lying about in the forest? Whilst he was wrestling with the awful possibilities that thought opened up, he heard men's voices and looked round to see Baladan returning. He was talking to Zabad. His voice was quiet, easy, friendly – and he had his arm round The Reaper's shoulder.

'He has not *run* away!' Maaz bellowed. 'When I tell my son what to do he does it!'

'Like he did the last time!' his neighbour, Ikesh, taunted.

Maaz's face was the colour of a beetroot and he hurled himself towards the man. But Halak had just come up, drawn by all the shouting outside Maaz's house, and before Maaz could get to Ikesh, the blacksmith had hold of him. 'I think you should calm down,' he told Maaz, in a low, rumbling voice.

Halak didn't often make suggestions, but when he did people usually followed them. Maaz let the tension out of his muscles, and the blacksmith released him.

'Tell it from the beginning,' Halak said. 'What's happened?'

Once he had stopped shouting, Maaz seemed uncertain and shy. He sat down heavily on the ground in front of his house, and the other two men joined him. Maaz stared away towards the river, glinting in the afternoon sun.

'I thought he was with Naama,' he said, vaguely.

'None of this would have happened in our old cottage – one room with everyone in it. We'd have known straight away if Ruel was missing. When we came in after the business with Baladan, I went into the big room, and Naama went into the kitchen. I thought Ruel was with her and Ezer in the kitchen. *She* thought he was with *me* in this stupid big room we can't even think of a name for. Then I went back out to work and didn't give Ruel a thought for the rest of the morning – as far as I was concerned he was safe at home with his mother. And now, I've just come back to find out Naama hasn't seen Ruel since Baladan went.'

Maaz seemed to pick up steam again at the mention of Baladan. 'It's obvious what's happened,' he said. 'All that about going to The Reaper was nonsense – he's just kidnapped Ruel and taken *him* to be a sacrifice for the gold he's stolen.'

'But he's a child,' Halak pointed out.

'What difference does that make to The Reaper?' Maaz snapped back. 'It's only us that said we'd never send a child. Anyway he's got the old woman too by the looks of it. I went straight to her place as soon as I knew the boy was gone, to see if he was there. He wasn't, and neither was she. He's kidnapped them both!'

That set Ikesh off again. If Zilla was gone, it just proved what he'd been trying to tell Maaz to begin with. It was ridiculous to say Zilla was kidnapped – if she was gone, it was obvious she'd have gone of her own free will. She was the nearest thing to a friend that Baladan had made in the village whilst he'd been there, so of course she'd have gone after him. And Ruel was *Zilla's* friend, so *he'd* have gone with *her* – he was a known runaway, in any case. It wasn't even worth discussing, let alone getting hot and bothered about. They were well rid of the mad woman – and if Ruel was gone, it was his own fault – he should do as he was told.

That was a foolish thing for Ikesh to say. All three men were on their feet again in a flash – Maaz struggling in Halak's grip shouting and shaking his fist at Ikesh, who was backing away towards his own house and shouting back. A little crowd soon gathered, and Maaz suddenly turned his attention on them.

'I want the man dead!' he screamed at them. He was beside himself, and they too started backing away as Maaz demanded that a search party go into the forest straight away to hunt Baladan down and string him up like a murderer. They felt very relieved that Halak was still holding Maaz as it seemed quite likely that he'd lay hands on some of them and drag them off with him there and then. Nobody wanted to wander around the forest with The Reaper and an angry Dragon on the loose. They'd made their decision on that when they'd all turned their backs on Baladan.

Someone else apart from Ruel and Zilla had been missing from the village since the morning. But there was no mystery about what had happened to him. It was Zethar, and Chilion had been crowing all day about what his friend was up to. Zethar might have let Chilion drag him away from Baladan that morning, but he hadn't gone to ground like everyone else. He'd told his friend that he was going to take cover in the trees and shadow Baladan to see what happened to him. And that's what he'd done, according to Chilion at least – he'd gone off into the forest that morning and hadn't been seen since.

It was just as Maaz seemed to have whipped himself into such a fury that he'd burst, that Zethar made his reappearance. He broke the treeline at a run, and seeing the crowd outside Maaz's house he headed straight for them, shouting out, as he came. Anyone who hadn't realised that something was going on downed tools when they saw Zethar running and yelling, and followed him towards the crowd. The young man had been running for miles, and his breath came in fits and starts, but he was desperate to get his message out.

'I saw him!' he gasped, 'with The Reaper. I saw Baladan with his arm round The Reaper – like long-lost friends. They've got Ruel and Zilla. They were there with a couple of other prisoners. Ruel was trying to help them escape, but before he could get them all untied Baladan and The Reaper came back. I saw it all.'

His breath ran out, and he simply stood there panting, but there was nothing more he needed to say. It was obvious to everyone that Baladan was a traitor, and something would have to be done. There was no order or discussion and everyone seemed to talk at once, but out of all the chaotic noise it became clear that someone would have to hunt Baladan down. The only trouble was that no one in the village but Maaz wanted to do it. Then Ikesh shouted out what the builders from Kiriath had said, and everyone wondered why they hadn't taken the suggestion before. It was simple – they would send a party to Baron Azal, tell him what had happened, and get him to send a squad of soldiers to pick up Baladan – after all, Baron Azal had a good reason to do it – Baladan had near enough insulted one of his officers already. With no Zilla to speak up for the King's rights over Hazar, the idea was agreed straight away.

The only sticking point came when Maaz insisted that something had to be done right then and there and that he was going to take a party into the forest straight away. It was Zethar who got them out of that one. He said that he was prepared to go back into the forest – he knew where Baladan was – and his friend Chilion would go with him.

Chilion looked as if he was going to faint, but he'd made such a big thing all day about Zethar being a hero and how he wished he'd gone with him, that he couldn't really refuse. Zethar said he'd need some runners to come with them so that they could keep relaying information back to the village about Baladan's position. On the strength of not having to do anything but run messages, five more young tearaways volunteered. Maaz was told by everyone that it was his responsibility to lead the party to go and see Baron Azal, and since Zethar and his group were already on their way back into the forest by then, he agreed. Ten minutes later, he set off for Kiriath with three other men and the foreman of the builders – and the rest of the village breathed a great sigh of relief.

CHAPTER SEVEN

'They need to know where we are.'

There was a pause whilst Chilion waited for some kind of response from his friend, but Zethar was as stubborn as he'd been for the whole week since they left Hazar, and kept silent.

'They'll think The Dragon's got us. They'll just give up on us. We might need them,' Chilion went on.

Still no response.

'We ought to try and link up with Baron Azal's men – they must have arrived from Kiriath by now. We ought to tell them where we are. We might as well work together from now on, don't you think?'

Again Chilion waited, but his friend said nothing.

'The rest of them won't put up with it for much longer. I'm surprised they're still with us, to be honest. If you leave it much longer, Zethar, they'll just go back anyway – the lot of them. They've had enough.'

This, at last, seemed to stir Zethar.

'They don't *know* the way back,' he muttered.

His friend hesitated to ask the question they'd all been wondering about for days, but at last he did. He'd had enough, too. 'Do you?' he said.

The answer was 'no', but Zethar wasn't going to say it. For a week they'd tried to pick up some trace of Baladan without the slightest whiff of success. Zethar had been confident to start with, but he had to admit to himself, if not to anyone else, that for the last two days he'd lost the last hint of an idea as to where they were. All the time, Chilion and the others had pestered him to send runners back to Hazar as he'd said he would. And he should have done – he realised that now. He should have gone on steadily – sending back word, making arrangements as to where he'd be by the time they returned, sticking to agreed plans and so on. But he was a bad loser, and it had seemed useless sending back the message that they'd found nothing. He wanted to send back news of success, not failure. So he'd led his men on and on – blundering about more and more wildly – and all for nothing. Here they were a week later, in the dead of night, camped in a forest with hardly any food and not a shred of hope left.

The campfire flickered. Zethar and Chilion kept watch whilst the other five were curled up in the grassy hollow where they'd made their camp for the night, unconscious from exhaustion. All of a sudden, Chilion knew there was someone else in the dell. There hadn't been the slightest warning sound, but someone was standing watching them all, not ten metres away. It was so unexpected that it was a moment before Chilion reacted. When he did, the little hollow turned into chaos. He shouted out, and straight away the men jumped up, but they were half asleep and didn't know what the danger was, so they staggered about, falling over each other and the fire, and caused more trouble to themselves than the intruder. The man could have done whatever he wanted – but all he seemed to want was to stand and watch. He let them get themselves together, and then he let them pull him towards what was left of the firelight. When they got him there, they saw that the man was Baladan – and that he was unarmed.

<hr>

'All right,' he said, 'now you've got me, what are you going to do with me?'

Everyone waited for Zethar, but they weren't expecting what he said. 'That depends on who you are,' he told Baladan.

The two looked each other in the eye and Zethar didn't flinch, but behind him there was confusion.

'What do you mean?' someone said, 'We *know* who he is.'

'He's a thief,' another added.

'A coward—'

'He's probably working for The Dragon.'

'Well,' said Baladan, keeping Zethar fixed with his eyes, 'there's your answer.'

They stared at each other for a moment longer, then Zethar turned away from him. 'I'm not sure,' he said. It wasn't clear who he was talking to. 'We need someone to fight The Dragon.'

The five who'd come with Zethar and Chilion had been lost in their heads as well as in the forest these last days. Chilion was right – they *had* had enough, but it was mostly because they didn't know what was going on any more. They felt that their leader was wrapped up in some private business of his own. They felt that he'd abandoned them, and so in their heads they'd been busy doing the same to him. They may not have realised too clearly what they were up to, but as they'd tramped on through the forest each of them had been sizing the others up, on the look-out for another leader – someone who'd try and get them out of this disaster area and back to their homes. If you'd asked them they'd probably have said that Thassi was the man. And it was Thassi who spoke up for them now.

'What are you on about?' he said. 'Dealing with The Dragon is Baron Azal's business – we sorted that out before we left Hazar. It's been decided.'

Zethar recognised the challenge at once, and turned on Thassi.

'Azal?' he said. 'Azal fight The Dragon? As far as I can make out he never fights anyone or anything.'

'Full marks to him then,' Thassi snapped back. 'He seems to keep Kiriath peaceful enough. At least he can *do* a job – which is more than can be said for you. You were supposed to be finding Baladan, and instead *he's* found *you*. You were supposed to be helping capture the man – and now I don't know *what* you think you're doing with him.'

Whether he realised it or not, Thassi had hit the target. That was just what Zethar didn't know himself, and having the accusation put straight like that winded him. Everything had been concentrated on finding Baladan – he hadn't thought further than that. He had to admit that whatever he might have said about sending word back to Hazar, there had been a blank in his mind about what would happen when they'd caught up with their man.

'I'm not sure you haven't been meaning to join up with him all this time,' Thassi went on. 'Is that what you've made us flog all this way to do?'

Confusion seemed finally to beat Zethar. 'I just wanted to find out who he was,' he said, quietly.

Thassi and Zethar had been facing up to each other, and everyone else had been concentrating on the confrontation. Now as the tension died they turned back to Baladan, and they saw he wasn't alone any more – Zabad was with him. As Ruel had said to Safir that time, Zabad was just a man – but he was a man with a dragon backing him up, and a lot of dead people to his name. As soon as they saw The Reaper, Zethar's men automatically shrank away from him. And maybe that's where Zethar got back his leadership, because he might have had a white-knuckle grip on his staff but he didn't budge a centimetre.

'I think you know Zabad,' Baladan said. 'He's camping with me and some other friends of mine a half hour's walk from here. I think you might know a couple of them as well.'

Baladan went on to describe the route to his camp in detail, making sure they couldn't possibly miss the way.

'Come to see us in the morning,' he said. 'Fight us, if that's what you want. Or join us. We'll have to see what happens if you decide to fight, but if you join us I promise you we'll fry The Dragon in its own fire and have rid of it for good.'

And with that, he and Zabad sank back into the shadows and away.

Morning saw Zethar at the head of his party, following the path to Baladan's camp. There'd been plenty of discussion after Baladan and Zabad had left the night before. The possibilities were clear – either Baladan was working with Zabad and was inviting them into a trap, or he was being straight with them. It came down to a matter of trust, and the fact that Baladan had turned up in their camp unarmed counted for a lot when they weighed it all up. Against that was the question of Zabad – no one had a clue how he fitted into things. Zethar hadn't tried to bully them – he'd seemed to be making his mind up as much as anyone – and that had helped them follow his lead when he finally came down in favour of joining Baladan.

Strangely enough, it was only when they'd decided that, that someone had suggested they could sidestep the whole thing by passing up Baladan's invitation altogether and just sending word back to Hazar that they'd found him – they could let the villagers decide what to make of it all. They'd dismissed that straight away – once they'd decided to join

Baladan, a strange excitement had seemed to take hold of them that they didn't want to give up. It could have had something to do with finding someone who sounded as if they knew what they were doing at last.

But they were still arguing as they made their way to Baladan's camp next morning. The question now was whether they should send word back to Hazar for a different reason – just to let the village know the decision they'd made.

'But what if they don't go along with us?' Thassi was saying. 'They weren't there last night – maybe they'll stick to wanting to kill Baladan, and all we'll have done is lead them to him.'

'We don't have to say where he is,' Chilion pointed out. 'I think telling them what's going on is the least we can do. They must be worried sick, not hearing from us for so long.'

'Are you sure it's not *you* that's worried sick?' Thassi asked him. 'Would you be thinking of volunteering to be the messenger by any chance?'

'Well, I—'

'I might point out that it's us lads that are supposed to be the runners – that's all we came on this trip for, remember? You're supposed to be second in command or something, aren't you?'

'I just thought – it's not going to be easy getting back – I thought maybe it ought to be me who has to go,' Chilion said.

'Or maybe you thought fighting The Dragon next to Baladan didn't sound too easy either.'

Thassi looked round for some support in jeering at Chilion, but they'd all been weighing up the dangers of being a messenger against the dangers of going on to meet The Dragon, and there was no one who felt like calling Chilion a coward just then.

The argument was knocked on the head by Zethar.

'You can all shut it!' he barked. 'There won't be *anyone* going back to Hazar.'

'Why? What do you mean?' Thassi asked.

'Nobody knows the way.'

'But, don't you...' Thassi's voice trailed off.

'I told you – *nobody* knows the way.' And Zethar stomped ahead, swiping out viciously at the undergrowth, and bruising himself badly against the branches.

Baladan's directions were clear, and they found him without any problems. He was waiting for them just where their path hit the glade he was camped in.

'Well, what's it to be – friend or foe?' he asked.

They noticed he was still unarmed.

'Not foe, anyway,' Zethar told him.

'If you're not against us, we'll take it you're for us – for the time being, at least.'

'If you say so.'

'Good man. I've been waiting for you.' Baladan looked round the whole of Zethar's group. 'I've been waiting for each one of you. You're welcome – come and join us.' He led them into the glade where Ruel and Zilla were busy getting breakfast ready. 'I think you know these two already,' he said. Then he pointed out a couple of women, one standing guard at each of the other two entrances to the glade. 'They're Rizpa and Lexa from Maon,' he said. 'They can tell you about themselves later – but there's someone else you'd better hear from first,' and he pointed to where a figure sat huddled on a tree trunk, in the centre of the camp. Although it was warm, he had a dark cloak wrapped around him with the hood up, casting his face into shadow.

It was almost as if he was hiding, but every one of them recognised The Reaper.

Baladan gestured for them to go to Zabad, but no one moved. There were ugly, threatening murmurs, but when Zabad flicked his eyes up at them for an instant their hearts went cold and they shrank back. The same as the night before, it was Zethar who held his nerve. After a moment, he marched over to The Reaper and stood over him, quarterstaff braced for combat. None of the others came with him. Zabad stayed where he was, bent over, face hidden in his hood.

'Speak then,' Zethar said. 'If you've got anything to say for yourself, spit it out.'

Slowly, Zabad sat up straighter and, pushing back his hood, he looked into the young man's face. There was a gasp from Zethar's party as they finally got a clear sight of the man who had chased through their nightmares since they were children.

'Perhaps now you can see me close up, I'm a little older than you thought,' he said.

And it was true – deep lines were worn into his face like scars. But what was most shocking of all was the deadness in his eyes.

'Zilla knew me when I was your age – and before,' Zabad continued. His voice was slow and unsure of itself, as if he wasn't used to speaking. 'I didn't look so bad then.'

Gradually the others crept forward, until at last they stood in a semi-circle behind Zethar. Zabad ran those miserable eyes over their faces.

'I suppose you're not used to looking at old men,' he said. 'Have you ever wondered why Jarib's the only one in

Hazar? There *should* be old men in Hazar – but that generation's gone.' His head dropped forward and he stared at the ground. 'And a dozen times every day I wish that I was gone with them,' he muttered.

'Sit with him,' said Baladan's voice, quietly behind them.

Again they hesitated. A mixture of fear and hatred seemed to lock their bodies rigid. Then Thassi lowered himself stiffly to the ground, and one by one, the others followed suit, but they didn't sit close to Zabad, and their hands were on their weapons.

Zabad continued to stare at the ground as he told them his story. 'We marched out bold as brass,' he said – 'full of hope – to put an end to The Dragon. Ten of us there were – armed to the teeth with everything we could find. This was long before Hanan and all his talk about the King – we didn't need any promise of help from the King. Not us – we didn't need help from *anyone*. That's the kind of fools we were.'

He raised his head, and there was a horror in his face that made it painful to look at. 'Have you ever seen a dragon?' he said. 'Only in your nightmares I expect. Well, imagine something a hundred times worse than that – towering over you so it blocks the sky, stinking like a hill of dead bodies, scales as thick as stone slabs, claws like scythes, roaring as if the earth's being torn apart, fire and smoke swirling round you like a flood, and everything happening faster than a snake can strike. Nine of us died in the blink of an eye – before they could draw breath to scream they were gone. I was the only one it didn't kill. It pinned me down with the point of a claw and gave me a choice – live as its servant, or die on the spot with my friends. I made a mistake – I chose to live. I chose to live and bring death to others, and hatred on myself.

'I've been a prisoner, a slave, for nearly thirty years – until Baladan found me and promised to kill The Dragon. For the first time in all those years he gave me hope and a taste of freedom.'

'What right have you to hope and freedom?' Zethar snapped. 'Think of all the people you've taken to be killed – what freedom have *they* got?'

Zabad stared at the ground again. 'I've no right to anything,' he acknowledged, 'least of all to the only thing that really *would* make me free – forgiveness. But Baladan says even that is possible.'

They turned to Baladan in astonishment, but what they saw in his face silenced the angry words that were about to burst out of them. Although he was by far the younger man, Baladan was looking at Zabad with the expression of a father watching over an injured child.

'I don't dare ask for forgiveness,' Zabad said. 'All I beg is that you trust Baladan. He's our only hope.'

Before anyone could reply there was a scuffle at the edge of the glade and everyone's attention swung away from Zabad. They saw Rizpa struggling with a man at the treeline. Lexa was running over to her sister, and the pair of them started dragging him into the camp. He looked to be a soldier and he was wearing a uniform that anyone who lived in the forest villages would have recognised: a surcoat of red and white quarters – Baron Azal's colours. Straight away, Zethar thought the worst and was on his feet. He raced over and grabbed the man, shaking him like a doll.

'How far behind are they?' he demanded. 'How many men has Azal sent? How are they armed? Tell me or you're dead!'

The man gazed at him dumbly, and Zethar pulled his fist back to punch him in the face. But the blow didn't land. Baladan was there and had snatched hold of Zethar's forearm quicker than you could blink.

'The man's injured,' he said, 'and exhausted.'

'Azal's men are in the forest,' Zethar explained, impatiently. 'They were sent for when we left Hazar. They're after you – they could be here any minute.'

'I know,' Baladan told him, calmly. 'I know all about it, and where they are – and it's nowhere near here.'

'But how? I haven't told you.'

'Zethar, I *do* need you – but not to tell me about Azal. Just look at this man – he's not one of the Baron's search party – look at the state of him.'

It was true. The man's surcoat was ragged and torn. He looked filthy and half starved. And, as Baladan had said, he was clearly injured – his arm was hanging limp by his side, wrapped in a bandage of pale brown cloth. By this time, everyone in the camp had gathered round, including Ruel. When the boy caught sight of the bandage he jumped for the man and nearly did him as much damage as Zethar had meant to.

'Where did you get it?' he yelled, tugging at the bandage. The man still looked dumb – almost unconscious. Desperately, Ruel turned to Baladan. 'Make him tell me where he got it!' he shouted.

'What is it, dearie?' said Zilla, pushing to the front.

Ruel was flapping a loose bit of the bandage, and calling out, 'It's Safir's – look – it's Safir's!'

'The man's not fit to tell anyone anything just now,' Baladan told him. 'Let him rest and eat, then he can tell us everything.'

Ruel had to be patient half the morning before Baladan allowed the man to be questioned. The soldier slept on a mattress Baladan had made for him out of sacks stuffed with bracken; and it was only when he'd had a good rest and eaten that Baladan let everyone gather round and hear what he had to say. The first thing he cleared up was that, sure enough, he wasn't one of the search party out hunting for Baladan – he didn't even know anything about them. But it turned out that he *was* from Kiriath. He was squire to Sir Achbor, one of Baron Azal's knights. Or at least he *had* been. He was a runaway now. He'd been on the run, living rough, for months – as they could tell by the state he was in.

'What are you running from?' Zethar asked him. 'Are you a murderer – a thief – an outcast?'

'I might be an outcast now,' the squire answered. 'But when I left, I cast *myself* out. I just couldn't stand living in Kiriath any more. You've no idea what it's like.'

'I thought it was supposed to be very nice,' said Zilla, 'peace and quiet and nobody starving.'

'Oh, there's *peace* all right,' the man told her, 'so much of it, it could send you crazy! Nothing ever happens. It's like dreamland. You could die of boredom. In fact, I think most people have. They look pretty dead to me, anyway. And the knights! I don't know how they can give themselves the name! All they ever do with their armour is polish it, and the only time they ever ride is to hunt. It was driving me mad – so I decided to go off in search of adventure.'

'It looks as if you found it,' said Lexa, pointing at his arm.

He had let them give him food and drink, but so far he hadn't let anyone touch his wound. He looked down at his useless arm with despair on his face.

'That put an end to my adventures before they'd even started,' he said. 'I got it almost as soon as I set off, and it won't heal no matter what I put on it. I've been good for nothing ever since – I can hardly manage to grub enough food together to keep myself alive, let alone go adventuring.'

They all wanted to know how he'd got his wound, so he told them the story. Apparently, he'd been camped in a clearing in the forest one day, a bit like the one they were in just now, when he'd heard the beat of wings coming up from the west.

'I thought it was a flock of swans to start with,' he said. 'It was loud, and swans have the loudest wings I'd ever heard before. But this just kept getting louder and louder. I realised something huge was coming and I jumped up with my sword in my hand – though what good I thought that was going to be, I don't know. The noise was getting tremendous, like a giant pair of bellows blowing in the sky – Whum! Whum! Whum! – then I saw it – it was The Dragon.

'I suppose you could say it looked quite beautiful in a way – deep, shiny green against the blue sky, with these huge wings reaching up and pushing down, just like a great big bird. But the most amazing thing was that there was a young woman riding on its back. I thought maybe they were friends for a minute – then she looked down and saw me. I don't know whether it was the colours of my coat, or the sun on my chain mail or what, but something must have caught her eye because all of a sudden she was waving, and it wasn't happy waving, I can tell you – she was desperate. She was yelling, then she was tearing at her dress, and the next thing I knew there was a strip of it floating down through the air. Straight away, The Dragon was on to what was happening. Its long neck twisted back and it took everything in – the young woman shouting, the falling bit of cloth, me on the ground.

'It stuck its wings out stiff and glided round in a huge arc over the clearing, then it tucked them in and zoomed down like a giant hawk. I thought it was coming for *me*, but then I realised it was the cloth it was after. It let loose a tiny jet of flame at it – just like spitting – and it must have thought it'd got a bull's eye, because it beat its wings again and soared straight up and away. The thing was though, it missed. There must have been a little breath of a breeze at the last minute – just made the cloth twist to the side before the flame hit it – and instead of getting the bit of the young woman's dress, that spit of fire hit me – right on the arm.'

Ruel was beside himself. 'I *told* you!' he was saying. 'I *told* you Safir was alive. She's been leaving us a trail to find her – bits of her dress – we just have to follow the trail.'

Everyone in the camp knew about Ruel and Safir and everyone was desperate to shield the boy from disappointment. Gentle voices started to point out that the squire had been wounded months ago. The young woman on The Dragon's back would probably be long dead by now. How could he even know that it *was* Safir on The Dragon's back?

Baladan had gone quietly to his horse whilst this discussion was going on. He came back with the great sword across his arms.

'Look,' he said, and he stretched out the material still tied to the scabbard, holding it against the strip wrapped round the squire's arm. There was no doubting it – the material was the same. There was even some of the same pattern of flowers that Safir had so carefully stitched onto the poor brown cloth to try and bring a bit of colour into their lives.

CHAPTER EIGHT

ow that he had pulled the bandage loose, the squire seemed ready to let his wound see the light of day. Zilla carefully unwrapped his arm, and as soon as the material from Safir's dress was off, Ruel snatched it. It was foul – crusted with dried pus and blood in places, and wet with fresh stuff in others – but still Ruel had to have it. He dashed straight off into the trees to the little rivulet that was giving the camp its water. He laid the precious strip in the icy stream and carefully worked away at it until all the filth was gone.

Meanwhile, the group gathered round the squire were trying hard to hide the fact that they felt like vomiting at the sight of his arm. From his elbow to his wrist was just a mess – raw flesh with yellow and green slime running out of it. It must have been giving the man agony all this time. Zilla started asking him about what herbs and leaves and mosses he'd tried on it, but Baladan interrupted her.

'There's nothing growing in the forest that'll heal a dragon's burn,' he said. 'It'll fester and rot the whole body. There's only one thing to do.'

And with that he drew the great sword from its scabbard.

Ruel was just coming back with the dripping cloth in his hand as the scabbard dropped empty to the ground. It was the first time he'd seen Baladan's sword unsheathed and he stopped dead in his tracks to stare. It was simply the most beautiful thing he'd ever seen. The blade was so pure and shiny that it made ripples of light flow over everything round it, the way sunlight comes off the surface of a full water bucket. But the most amazing thing was the size of it. It was so long that when Baladan put the point on the ground, the golden hilt came up to his chest. Each of the cross parts of the hilt was the length of his forearm, and the handle part was long enough to get a good grip with two hands, even fully armed with the metal gauntlets Ruel knew a knight would wear. There were no two ways about it – it was a knight's battle sword. Ruel looked at Baladan closely and thought, He must be a knight then. It was the first time the idea had struck him. He'd got used to thinking of Baladan as a mystery – someone who didn't fit into any kind of category. Not that putting the label 'knight' on him made him any less mysterious – if that's what he was, he was a strange one – stranger than any kind of knight that Ruel had ever heard of.

Ruel wasn't the only person staring at the sword. The squire couldn't take his eyes off it either but for a different reason. He knelt down with a wince of pain and stretched his arm out until it rested on one of the logs they'd been using as benches. His eyes were big as a frightened rabbit's, and it was obvious he thought Baladan's answer to his wound was to chop off his arm at the elbow. Everybody else did too, and one or two closed their eyes as Baladan swung the sword high in the air, making the reflections that had been gently rippling over the bystanders suddenly light up the whole glade. But instead of bringing the blade crashing down, Baladan held it above his head – every muscle in his arms straining as he balanced the weight of metal there, a palm's width above his skull. When he brought the blade down again, it came down slowly and gently, until it lay flat across the wound. He tilted it slightly in the sun, and the reflection was so powerful that everyone had to close their eyes or put their arms across their faces.

When they looked again, Baladan had taken his sword away. There was a second of stunned silence, then everyone was talking at once and grabbing hold of the squire's arm, twisting and turning it in disbelief. It was completely healed. The squire was behaving like everyone else – treating his arm like some object that didn't belong to him, joining in with the bending and poking. He kept saying, 'It doesn't hurt, it doesn't hurt a bit' – as if he wanted them to be as rough as they liked with him.

Baladan stepped out of the way to clean his sword, put it back in its scabbard, and return it to its place with the rest of his equipment. Then he came back and put his hand on the squire's shoulder.

'Go on your way now,' he said. 'Be thankful that you ran into us. And whatever you do, don't tell anyone what happened to you here.'

It was spoken gently, but there was no mistaking that it was an order. The man looked around at everyone as if he wanted to say something, but nothing came. He looked at Baladan, but Baladan just twitched his head towards the trees as if he was telling him to get a move on. A moment's more hesitation, then the squire simply turned and ran.

Zethar had obviously been itching to speak. And as the squire disappeared he couldn't hold himself back any longer.

'Are you off your head?' he asked Baladan. 'What if he bumps into Azal's men? Crashing around like that they're bound to pick him up if he comes within half a kilometre of them. Then he'll blab and give us away.'

'That's why I told him not to say anything,' Baladan replied.

'And you think he's going to take any notice of that?' Zethar asked. 'Why on earth didn't you keep the man with us?'

Baladan looked at him hard, then at the other eleven gathered round him in the glade: Ruel and Zilla, Rizpa and Lexa, Zabad, Chilion, Thassi and the four others.

'*You're* the ones that I need,' he said. 'Just you – no one else.'

'I don't understand what you're worried about, anyway,' Lexa put in. 'Why are Baron Azal's men such a problem? If they find us, we'll just explain that Baladan's going to fight The Dragon. Everybody wants someone to do that, don't they?'

'You don't know the man that's leading them,' Chilion explained. 'It's Ruel's father. He's got it in his mind that Baladan's kidnapped his son and he wants to tear him to bits. There won't be any reasoning with him.'

'But we don't *need* to reason,' Lexa went on. 'Ruel's *here*, safe and well, all we have to do is *show* him.'

'Zethar's right,' Baladan told them. 'There *is* danger, but I think you'll find that it's Baron Azal's men who won't be convinced if they find us, not Ruel's father.'

'But why?' Ruel asked. 'Aren't they against The Dragon too?'

'They do what their master tells them,' Baladan replied. Which didn't explain anything, as far as Ruel was concerned. But he didn't have time to argue. 'We must move fast now,' Baladan was saying. 'It's time. We have to strike camp and go.'

'Go where?' Chilion asked.

Baladan looked at him as if he was stupid.

'To the mountain,' he said, 'where else?'

⁕

Five men from Hazar and ten men-at-arms from Kiriath were gathered in a huddle in the depths of the forest. In the centre of the huddle were their two leaders – an officer of Baron Azal's guard, and Maaz. The leaders were taking it in turns to question a man. Not that he needed any pushing to spill the beans. The man was the squire. He'd seemed overjoyed to run into the party, even though the soldiers were from Kiriath; and just as Zethar had predicted, he was now pouring out everything that had happened to him almost faster than his listeners could take it in.

Although the squire's words were wild and excited, it was obvious to Maaz that the man was talking about Baladan, and when they eventually got the squire to calm down a bit and describe the rest of the group, it was clear that Baladan not only had Ruel and Zilla with him, but also Zethar and his men – and it even sounded as if Zabad, the dreaded Reaper might be there. The men from Hazar couldn't make any sense out of this, and the squire couldn't help them – he hadn't a clue who the people were who'd looked after him, or what they were up to.

'I never did trust Zethar,' Maaz said at last. 'All he's ever been interested in is himself, ever since he was a boy. Just think of all the fights and arguments he used to get into. He was never too bothered whose side he was on as long as he got a chance to bust a few lips and make a name for himself.'

'What are you saying?' one of the Hazar men asked, 'That he's joined Baladan?'

'That's exactly what I'm saying.'

'But what about the rest of them?'

Maaz gave a hard little laugh and tossed his head. 'That Chilion just goes whichever way the wind blows,' he said. 'Why else do you think Zethar wanted Chilion with him in the first place? And the rest of them haven't got a half brain between them. With Chilion behind him, Zethar could bully them into anything he wanted. I bet he planned to join Baladan from the start. He was keen enough to go after him – before any of us even had time to think properly. Working for The Dragon would probably suit the lot of them down

107

to the ground. It's just an excuse to spend all their time stirring up trouble.'

The men from Hazar weren't convinced. Some of them thought Zethar might have joined Baladan because he'd found out that Baladan really *did* mean to fight The Dragon. But then Maaz came back to the story of the squire's healed arm.

'It's obvious,' he said. 'This man's from Kiriath. The Dragon respects Baron Azal's people, and so do its servants, that's *why* Baladan healed him. And it's because he's The Dragon's servant that he knew *how* to heal him.'

The men wavered at this. When it came to mysterious happenings they were way out of their depth. They got frightened and could be made to believe almost anything. But they were still uncertain. Maaz had been like a lunatic since Ruel had gone, and he'd been driving them on through the forest even harder than the military men these last days. He had just one thing on his mind – to find Baladan and destroy him. You couldn't quite trust the judgement of someone like that.

In the end, it was the soldiers who sorted it out.

'*You* can do what you want,' the officer told the Hazar men, 'but we have our orders.'

'I thought your orders were to help us,' one of the villagers said.

'Our orders are to bring this Baladan character into Kiriath. You can help us or not – that's up to you.'

The officer questioned the squire carefully until he was sure of the way to Baladan's camp and then set off at once. It was half a day's march away and they couldn't waste a minute. Maaz went with the soldiers without question, and after a moment's hesitation, the other four villagers tagged on behind.

When they finally got near to the glade that had been

Baladan's camp, the officer told the villagers to stay where they were and he led his men creeping forward, bush by bush and tree trunk by tree trunk, aiming to surprise the lookouts Baladan would have in position. Maaz had been impressed with the soldiers from the beginning: Baron Azal had obviously not sent a bunch of idiots out to Hazar – these men had proved several times over the past days that they were crack woodsmen. Azal must want Baladan pretty badly, Maaz thought – just as badly as he wanted him himself.

Maaz's thoughts were disturbed by a sudden shout. It was the officer's voice, and he was cursing loudly. Maaz and the others jumped up, quarterstaffs at the ready, and ran forward. But they didn't find fighting in Baladan's glade. They didn't find anything at all. It was empty. The officer was standing at the edge of the little grassy clearing, staring up at the sky and swearing at the passing clouds as if it was their fault he'd arrived too late to catch his man. He punched a nearby tree with his leather-gloved fist, then swore again and shook his hand to ease the pain.

But it's not easy to hide the trail made by thirteen people and a horse – especially from the kind of men Baron Azal had set on Baladan's track – and within minutes of finding the empty glade one of the soldiers shouted that he'd spotted signs of the route Baladan's people had taken. This was all they needed – all they'd ever needed throughout the time they'd been in the forest – just to hit on Baladan's trail. Once they had that, they'd never give up until they got him, the officer explained to Maaz. It was just a matter of time now. Although evening was coming on, they set off again at once and kept going until long after even Maaz had given up trying to make out the signs they were following.

Next day, they were up and away again before dawn – a silent, determined file. It was noon before the officer called a halt, and even then it was only to make a simple announcement.

'He's heading for the mountain,' he said.

Maaz and his men had been much more cautious than Zethar's party and had managed to hang on to a sense of where they were for most of their time in the forest. But now, even they were lost, so they should have been glad to get a clue as to their whereabouts – but mention of the mountain wasn't exactly welcome news. The villagers glanced anxiously at each other. And the Kiriath men didn't look too cheerful either – which Maaz found surprising, given that Baron Azal was the only person around who didn't seem worried about The Dragon.

'If you're right about him working for The Dragon,' the officer went on, 'then he must be making for his master's lair. Our only chance is to cut him off before he gets there.'

The pursuers set off again, and there was no more moving cautiously now, no more hiding their trail: the race to the mountain was on.

By mid-afternoon, even the soldiers were showing signs of tiredness; and the men of Hazar were exhausted. Panting, bleeding from cuts and scratches, and with their clothing shredded by branches and brambles, the party crouched in the cover of the last trees. They were there. A few strides ahead of them was the open ground that led to the first slopes of the mountain. They'd made it, but they hadn't caught Baladan. They hadn't even had a glimpse or a sound of him. Their only hope was that he and his party were resting at the mountain foot, or were still within reach on the lower slopes.

Silent as shadows, the men of Hazar and Kiriath materialised from the trees and stood facing the mountain in battle line, swords and staves at the ready. They screwed their faces up, dazzled by the light, and scanned the rocky slopes before them for signs of their prey. A rattle of loose stones made them start and grip their weapons, but no figure was scrambling up the broad band of scree that had started to shift away to their left. The stones settled again, leaving no other sound but the tumbling of a mountain stream. It made them shiver. Maaz noticed that there were no birds singing, and there was a chill in the air despite the sun. Just standing that close to the mountain turned your heart cold. There wasn't so much as a bush for cover, and they had a clear view as far as the crags high above that marked the start of the real climb to the summit. No living thing was moving on all that great ramp of shrivelled grass and shingle – not even a goat.

They split into two parties and set off in opposite directions, scouting the whole way round the base of the mountain to see if Baladan was going up another way. But when they met up again after a weary hike, neither group had seen the slightest sign. Those high crags were like a castle wall around the peak of the mountain, and Baladan must have already got beyond them.

'Aren't we going up after him?' said Maaz, but his voice sounded weak, as if he was hoping for someone to think of a good reason why not.

And before the officer could answer, he got one. It was a sound like nothing any of them had ever heard before. When they told people about it later, they called it a roar, but the word did nothing to describe what they heard just then. It was like the earth being torn apart and the whole mountain falling in rubble on their heads. The ground did actually seem to shake underneath their feet, and although the mountain stayed in one piece, a great cloud of black smoke began to roll down from the top of it in a wave.

Like wild animals bolting, all but one of them ran for the trees. Only Maaz stood firm against the fear, but his heart was leaping inside him as if it wanted to rip itself out of his chest. Through the terror in his mind came astonishment that the soldiers of Kiriath were running as well as the men from Hazar.

'Hey!' he bellowed after them. 'You're supposed to be dragon fighters! Come back!'

But they were running in blind panic, their officer in the lead, and didn't even look over their shoulders, let alone answer. Maaz stood alone, and then there was another roar. He knew in his heart that everything was lost. His son was lost as his daughter had been lost: it was all over. He didn't run. There didn't seem any point. He straightened his shoulders, turned his back on the mountain, and walked slowly towards the trees.

Way above the line of the crags, not far from the summit, and well out of sight of anyone at the foot of the mountain, was a ledge about ten paces deep. The mountain shook, and thick, stinking smoke rolled past Baladan's twelve. They were huddled at the back of the ledge to get out of the way of the boulders that were bouncing down from the heights above them. Baladan himself was asleep. He'd told them all to rest on the ledge before their final climb, and lying down a short distance away from them had gone to sleep at once. The first roar had brought the twelve to their feet, and the second had sent them huddling against the rock, but neither had had the slightest effect on Baladan.

They shouted and yelled at him, but still he didn't stir. Zilla and Ruel clung tightly to each other. Zilla cradled the boy against her as if he was much younger than he was, but he buried his face in her clothing and didn't complain. A few moments after the second roar, the smoke began to clear a bit, but the mountain still shook, as if a huge forge had been set going deep inside it. Zilla looked out over the miles of forest spread underneath them. Now that they were on the mountain, she could work out which direction Hazar was in, and could even find the break in the trees and the trails of smoke that marked the place she'd lived in all her life. This far away mountain had always just been a part of the scenery. It was strange to think that now it was going to be the place where she died. She didn't have any doubt about that. She'd lived so long and seen so much that she often used to tell Ruel that nothing frightened her any more – and she'd meant it. But now, with the mountain still shaking under her and the roaring still echoing in her ears, she was as terrified as a child.

Minutes passed. There was trembling and rumbling beneath their feet, but no more roaring. At last Rizpa found the courage to move and went over to shake Baladan awake. She told him what had happened and how terrified they were. Baladan stretched and stood up straight. He looked them over, still crouched at the back of the ledge. Ever since they'd left camp for the mountain, Chilion had been tormenting himself with doubts. He'd been coming to the same conclusions as Maaz about the healing incident, and now Baladan's cool stare after all the commotion on the mountain pushed him over the edge. 'I know what you're up to,' he burst out. 'This is all a trap. You've brought us here to feed to The Dragon. I'm going.' And he lurched to his feet.

Baladan seemed unimpressed. 'You can *all* go,' he told them. He pointed to the south-west. 'There's Hazar. You know where you are now. Zilla will lead you.' And he looked her in the eye, calm and steady. 'The Dragon's angry,' he said. 'It knows someone's on the mountain. It wants us to go. Perhaps you'd better – it's up to you.'

The thing Zilla wanted most in the world just then was to get off the mountain and be on her way home. But then she remembered how she'd followed Baladan into the forest when he'd set out on this mission, the only one from the village to come with him, until Ruel had turned up. And she remembered how Baladan had said he'd rather have her with him than an army. She took a deep breath and stood up.

'I'm not going,' she said.

She had hold of Ruel's hand, and was gripping it so hard it hurt, but he managed not to make a sound.

<hr/>

An hour later, when they were within sight of the summit, Baladan stopped and led them into the shelter of an overhanging rock. There had been more roaring, smoke, and falling boulders, but no one had left the twelve.

'The Dragon knows *someone's* here,' Baladan said. 'So now we'd better tell it *who*!'

Baladan had had to leave Hesed in the forest: he was hidden where Maaz and his party would never find him. All he'd brought with him to meet The Dragon was his sword, slung over his shoulder and hanging down his back; and a long pouch, hanging from his belt. He opened the pouch now and took out a small golden horn. He stepped away from the shade of the overhang and raised it to his lips. The note that came out was surprising: deeper and much more powerful than seemed likely from such a small instrument. When Baladan lowered the horn again its note seemed to hang in the air a long time. As it finally faded away, so did the shaking that had kept going under their feet since The Dragon's first roar.

'Now,' said Baladan.

He signalled to them and warily the twelve crept out from the overhang to join their leader. Ruel's fingers were shaking as he tried to get a grip on the rock face that led to the summit, but up he went after Baladan. One by one, his companions hooked toes and fingers into crannies and crevices and began to climb – even Zilla. Soon they were all spread out across the twenty metres of rock that stood between them and The Dragon's lair. It wasn't hard climbing, but just the brush of a dragon's wing would have sent the lot of them tumbling like spiders blown off a wall. And they had no threads to save them. Ruel concentrated on each handhold to drive the thought from his mind. What they would find and what they would do when they reached the top, he couldn't imagine. He tried not to think beyond the next movement of hand or foot.

All too soon, the end of the climb drew near, and they saw Baladan haul himself over the top of the rock wall and disappear. With their leader out of sight, they seemed to freeze for an instant. It was Zethar who shook them into action again. With a grunt, he launched himself up the wall once more and in a few moments had followed Baladan over the top. Minutes later, all twelve were crouching with Baladan amongst a group of boulders that stood like guards at the top of the rock wall they'd just climbed. An open space stretched between them and the gaping mouth of The Dragon's cave. Ruel stared in horror across it. The scene looked like something that didn't belong to this world. The whole place was littered with burnt cinders; there were dozens of jagged, blackened rocks thrown around like broken teeth; bones were scattered everywhere – most turned grey by weathering and lichen, but some more fresh; and the place stank of every rotting thing in the world. Ruel felt suddenly hot and dizzy, and he retched.

At that very moment, there was a scream, a roar, a rush

of darkness, and something with the force of a hundred Halaks threw Ruel to the ground. He lay on his back, stunned, winded, staring above him with no understanding of what he saw. It was dark, and he seemed to be under a roof; but the roof was moving, and it was made of great green slates. Heat was melting him, stench drowning him; and with a deafening 'whum!' like a gigantic door slamming, the air seemed to press down on him until he felt he was going to be flattened. Then the roof lifted, light flooded in, and Ruel realised he was looking up at the underbelly and great leathery wings of The Dragon as it soared into the air.

Ruel expected to see Baladan, weapon in hand, braced for battle; but when his dazed eyes found their leader, he was standing in front of The Dragon's cave, sword still sheathed, hands on his hips, calmly watching the beast pulling away into the sky. And sure enough, it didn't bank round to attack but went on beating its wings with the deafening whum! whum! the squire had described and kept climbing ever higher without a backward look. On and on it flew, the sound of its wing beats gradually fading, until its body looked no bigger than a pigeon's and it disappeared at last into a fluffy white cloud.

There was a stunned silence, as one by one they picked themselves up, rubbed their bruises and stared into the empty sky. Ruel found himself instinctively looking round the nightmare scene on the mountain top for more strips of his sister's dress. But he felt muddled – in his heart he knew she wasn't there, and somehow he didn't think she ever had been.

It was Zabad who was the first one to find his voice again.

'That was too easy,' he said.

'You're right,' Baladan told him. 'You know your old master well enough to know it won't give up without a fight.'

He looked round at his little band. 'There's more work for us to do yet before the job's finished,' he said and he started off towards the cliff wall they had so recently climbed.

'Hang on a minute!' said Zethar. 'What about the treasure?'

'Time enough for that,' Baladan said. 'We've somewhere else to go first.'

'Where?' Zethar asked.

Baladan pointed to the east.

'There,' he said.

They all followed the line of his finger and in the distance they saw tiny white turrets, gilded roofs, spots of colour that were flags and pennants. It looked to Ruel like the King's castle of his dreams. It was the town of Kiriath.

CHAPTER NINE

There was a *whap* of flame as the man lit his sticks and the ring of children gathered round him jumped back with oohs and ahs. Quite a few of the grown-ups behind them gave a start too. But lighting the sticks up was nothing – next minute they were sailing though the air in an amazing tangle of flaming loops and swoops – one at a time, then in pairs; high, then low; now far from the man's body, making the crowd step even further back, now straight up and down above him. The juggler seemed to be surrounded by a storm of fire, but in the middle of it his body was completely still – only his arms were moving, never stopping, looking as if they didn't really belong to the rest of him.

'How does he *do* it?' Ruel asked, in an excited whisper.

'By getting burned a lot,' Baladan told him.

'But he's not getting burned at all.'

'Not now – he probably did when he was your age though.'

'Did he *really* start when he was my age?'

'To get that good, he'd have to.'

'Is he *very* good?' Ruel asked. He'd never seen a juggler before – or *any* of the sights they'd seen in Kiriath market that morning.

'*Very!*' Baladan said.

The two of them were at the front of the crowd – Baladan had seen to that – and Baladan was kneeling down amongst the children. Ruel took a quick sideways glance and for the first time since he'd known him, he saw Baladan's face lit up as if he was really enjoying himself.

'Just look at the way his arms are dancing,' Baladan said.

All Ruel had really been taking notice of were the fire sticks, but now that he looked hard at the juggler's arms he could see what Baladan meant. There was a rhythm and a pattern to the way they were moving, just like a dance.

'And his face – look how he's sweating!' Baladan went on.

He was certainly doing that – he looked as if someone had thrown a bucket of water over him. And Ruel noticed how tight his face was – all the rest of him seemed relaxed, but his jaws were clamped shut and his eyes were darting around following the sticks.

'Perhaps he's hot,' Ruel suggested.

'Oh he's that, all right,' Baladan laughed, 'but it's more than that – it's concentration. The houses of Kiriath could get up on their legs and walk away, and he'd never even notice.'

Ruel was so surprised he looked right away from the juggler, and found himself looking in Baladan's eyes. They were shining, and there were little laugh lines at the corners.

'Houses don't walk,' he said.

Baladan looked shocked. 'Don't they?' he said. 'Not even in Kiriath? I thought this was supposed to be a magic place!'

⚓

Sometimes Lexa was so embarrassed by her sister Rizpa that she wanted to dig a hole in the ground and hide in it. Just now, Lexa had stepped back from the little group of customers round the cheese stall and was pretending she wasn't *with* Rizpa. She could still hear her, though. Her sister was arguing with the stall keeper over the price of a cheese.

'Call that a cheese!' she was saying. 'It smells like something that's dropped out of a donkey's backside!

It's not worth *half* what you're asking for it.'

There was a lot of laughter from the other customers, and the stall keeper was getting cross.

'I'll have you know, I supply cheeses to Baron Azal,' he told her.

'Do you really! Well, I'll have *you* know, someone had better supply him with a doctor then, and quick!' Rizpa snapped back. More laughter.

The man was losing and he knew it. In the end he let Rizpa have the cheese at a knock-down price just to get rid of her.

'What's the point?' Lexa asked her when her sister came towards her, waving the cheese in the air like a prize. It was a flattened ball shape, golden yellow, and really did look fit for the Baron's table. 'I mean, it's not as if you couldn't afford what he was asking.' Before they'd left the mountain, Baladan had been into The Dragon's cave and got them all some gold for their trip to Kiriath – Rizpa could have afforded to buy the whole stall if she'd wanted to.

'What's the point?' Rizpa repeated. 'The *fun* of it – that's the *point*, my girl! Here, catch! Mmm, this is good!'

She'd hacked a chunk off, stuffing it in her mouth, and now she threw the rest of the cheese to her sister. Lexa couldn't help laughing. When she wasn't being desperately embarrassed by Rizpa, she loved her very much.

⚓

In the shade of a bright, red and white striped awning Chilion was turning a plate over and over. The stallholder was looking nervous – those big, rough hands might let the delicate circle of pottery go flying any minute. He wished these particular customers would move on quickly to the pots and pans stall next door – they'd be safer there.

'This is good stuff,' Chilion was saying to Zethar. 'Look at the pattern.'

'What do *you* know about it?' his friend asked, sarcastically.

'I'm telling you, it's good – so's this.' And he picked up a really fancy jug with a curly handle.

This was too much for the man behind the stall.

'Watch what you're doing, for heaven's sake,' he said, 'that's travelled across two seas to get here – it doesn't want to end up in bits on the ground.'

Zethar suddenly got hold of the edge of the stall and fixed the man with a dangerous glare.

'Listen,' he said, 'any more of that and the whole lot'll be bits on the ground.'

The man swallowed hard as his jugs and ornaments gave a gentle tinkle.

'All right! All right!' he said. 'Just be careful, that's all.'

'And you just be careful what you say to my friend,' Zethar warned.

Chilion was still busy looking at the jug. 'I'll have this,' he said, digging into his purse.

'Who for? Your mother?' Zethar joked.

Chilion looked a bit hurt. 'Yeah,' he said. 'Why not?'

<hr>

Thassi and his four friends had done a tour of the market. They'd never seen so many vegetables all in one place before. They didn't even know what some of them were *called*, never mind what they tasted like. One whole side of the market square was taken up with them – all set out in big straw baskets. The sellers sat here and there amongst them on wooden stools, with their leather money bags in their laps.

Then there was the meat section. The villagers of Hazar were vegetarian most of the time because they had no choice – meat was a rare treat as most of theirs went to the Dragon. But judging by these stalls you could eat meat every day of the week in Kiriath if you wanted to. There was fresh meat of every kind, hanging from beams under the butchers' awnings; and beside every stall there were big barrels full of pickled meat in salt water.

Looking at all that food made them hungry, and Thassi bought them a pie each from a woman with a basket, weaving her way through the crowd. They were herring pies, and Thassi asked her where the fish came from. She pointed to the castle on its hill above the town, and told him there was a river in the valley on the far side of it. It couldn't be the river that flowed through Hazar, because the woman said it was wide and deep enough for cargo boats to sail on. Apparently, they brought fish and all kinds of things in from far away places and unloaded them at a little harbour just below the castle walls. Baron Azal's men ran it all.

The thing that struck the five of them most about Kiriath market was the noise of it. The woman pie seller had an amazing voice: it boomed out as she walked on, shouting about her good herring pies, and almost deafened them. But she had to be loud because everyone else was shouting about what *they* had to sell. And that meant that the townspeople had to shout at each other to make themselves heard as they wandered round the stalls. Then there was singing and shouting from the Tavern, and cheering from the wrestling match going on in front of it. And a group of minstrels were playing for all they were worth in the middle of the square – the bagpipes and drums were making themselves heard well enough above the racket, but you couldn't hear the little harp and the fiddle until you were quite close. It was like a big party, and the pie seller had told them it happened on this day every other week.

If the noise the people were making wasn't enough, there were animal sounds too to add to the din. The five friends ended up eating their pies by a set of wicker pens at the far end of the square that were full of sheep. They were baaing frantically, packed tight and vibrating with fear. Men were poking them with sticks and discussing the pros and cons of buying this, that or the other breed. Thassi and his friends discussed how good it would be to have any kind of sheep at all back in Hazar.

***

'That's Baron Azal's stall,' said Zabad, pointing.

'What kind of a stall do you call that?' Zilla asked him. 'It's more like a little house.'

And she was right. All the market stalls were made of bits of wood, so they could be taken down at the end of the day. But what Zabad was pointing at had plaster and timber walls and was obviously there to stay.

'What does he sell in there, anyway?' she asked.

'Good question. Space, I suppose. Anyone who has a stall or does anything in the market has to pay a tax to Azal – that's where they go to pay it.'

Azal's tax house was where the main street of Kiriath led into the square. Zilla and Zabad walked past it and up the street, away from the market. They were the oldest of the twelve, and the noise and crowds were getting too much for them. The street led on up to the castle, and there was a stretch of grass between the last buildings of the town and the ramp up to the castle drawbridge. Zilla and Zabad sat down here to rest in the shade of a tree. Nearby were two bell tents pitched on the grass – they were obviously something to do with the market, but they only had a few customers gathered in little huddles outside them. Zilla was puzzled – the customers looked rather nervous. Suddenly there was a strangled scream from the tent on the left.

'What on earth was that?' she asked.

'Torture,' Zabad said.

A few moments later a man came out of the tent and spat a mouthful of blood onto the grass, then staggered away holding a cloth to his mouth. A man came to the flap of the tent, wearing an apron covered in red stains. His sleeves were rolled up, and he had big muscly forearms. He took some money from his next customer and led him into the shadows of his tent.

'Barber-surgeon,' Zabad explained, 'arm off, tooth out, or haircut – you pay your money and you take your choice.'

'What about the other tent?' Zilla asked. 'It's all young women queuing for that.'

'That's the fortune teller.'

They laughed but it was half hearted. These two strange tents seemed to change their lighthearted mood, and a serious atmosphere started to grow between them. That often happened when Zabad was around. The change from thinking of Zabad as the nightmare Reaper to thinking of him as just another victim of The Dragon was hard enough for any of them to make. But Zabad himself seemed to find more difficulty than all of them in handling the new situation. Sometimes he would wander away and spend hours on his own – at times like that it was usually only Zilla who could get him back, and on occasions Baladan alone who could do it.

'What is it, dearie?' Zilla asked, at last.

'I don't know how you can call me that,' he said, not looking at her.

'What – "dearie"? I say it to everyone.'

'I mean, after what I've done.'

There was more silence, then another scream from the surgeon's tent.

'Tell me what you think of me – honestly,' he asked her.

'Honestly, dearie – I feel sorry for you, truly I do.'

'But what about all those people that I – I took to that Thing?'

'I feel sorry for them too.'

'What do the others think?'

'Don't worry about them, dearie. As long as Baladan's around, you're safe enough.'

He looked at her, surprised.

'I wasn't really meaning that,' he said. 'Just looking at that fortune teller's tent got me thinking of the future. I was wondering if she could tell me how long it would be before you could all forgive me.'

They watched a young woman come out of the tent with a funny secret smile on her face, then run back into town. Another one went in with shifty looks all around as if she was worried someone might be spying on her.

'The only thing you'll find out in there is how easy it is to give away good money for rubbish,' Zilla said, 'but I'll tell you a piece of truth for free – whatever time it takes, you'll have been forgiven long before you can forgive yourself.'

A little while later, Zilla and Zabad saw two people they knew coming towards them. It was Baladan and Ruel.

'Someone got toothache?' Baladan asked, as he came up to them.

'Heartache, more like,' Zilla said quietly, nodding towards Zabad.

'Zabad – a job for you,' Baladan told him, 'for both of you, in fact. Ruel and I are going up to the castle. See if you can find everyone else and tell them to meet us at the

Tavern this evening. Have something to eat whilst you're waiting for us.'

And the pair of them set off up the slope to the drawbridge. Zilla watched them go, and noticed the easy way they were talking together. At one point, Baladan put his hand on the boy's shoulder as he pointed something out up ahead. Of all of them, Ruel was the one Baladan seemed to have got closest to, and Zilla had to admit it gave her a twinge of jealousy – although quite which one she was jealous of, she wasn't sure.

It was a fine castle and no mistake – smooth, dressed stone walls that looked white from a distance, gilded cones on the tops of its turrets, and bright flags everywhere. It had well designed battlements, cleverly arranged arrowslits, and a massive gatehouse that could keep an army out. But you could tell it was a long time since it had seen any action. Baladan pointed to the place where the drawbridge rested on the ground to make the bridge across the moat.

'Look at the way that's bedded into the earth,' he said to Ruel. 'There's turf growing over the edge of it! You'd have to *dig* that out to shift it. I doubt if it's been raised for years.'

There was a bell chain hanging by the great wooden doors to the castle and Baladan told Ruel to pull it. After a few minutes, the doors swung open – no scraping of any bolts or locks – and the gatekeeper, an old man with a red face and white hair, stood barring their way. He had a fluffy white beard too, so his face smiled at them out of a complete circle of white. He didn't look exactly ready for battle either. He wore chain mail and a bright soldier's surcoat in Azal's colours, but even Ruel could probably have knocked him over without working up much of a sweat.

'Oh, hello there! Come in, come in!' he said, standing aside at once. ' Now what can I do for you?' He looked from one to the other of them as if he was desperate to be some help. 'Would you care for a drink, either of you?' he said, and without waiting for an answer, he turned his back on them and shuffled away inside. Ruel looked at Baladan. He was smiling and winked at Ruel, nodding to him to follow the old man.

The great doors opened onto a passage through into the castle courtyard, and on the left of the passage was the door to the old man's gatehouse. They followed him through it and he settled them in a couple of comfortable wooden armchairs whilst he fussed about getting them some nettle beer. He'd got himself a cosy little place – whitewashed walls, with a couple of colourful wall hangings showing hunting scenes; good quality dark wood table and sideboard; and a big window with real glass in it, opening onto the castle courtyard. Ruel could see lots going on out there – squires in bright coats leading horses in and out of the stables, and ladies in beautiful silk gowns walking about with their maids.

'Now then,' the old gatekeeper said, when they were served with their drinks, 'what was it you were wanting?'

'I'd like to see your master, Baron Azal,' Baladan told him. 'Tell him Baladan has come to slay The Dragon.'

The old man spluttered on his beer. 'Well I never,' he said. 'Well, well, well. Now there's a strange message and no mistake. Are you sure you're in the right place, young man?' Baladan just smiled, so the gatekeeper heaved himself onto his feet and made for the door. 'Oh well, back in a jiffy then,' he said. 'Oh – er – would you mind looking after the door for me while I'm gone? If anyone rings just – er, just ask them to wait here for me. You can get them a drink if you like.'

He was back in a few minutes, beaming all over his face. 'There you are,' he told them, 'I knew what he'd say. He says "not today, thank you" – or words to that effect.'

'What exactly *did* he say? If you don't mind me asking,' Baladan enquired.

'Oh. Oh, well now, what was it? Oh yes – "The Dragon doesn't come into these parts, so you'll have to look for it elsewhere" – something like that.'

'Well, tell Baron Azal I'd still like to talk to him,' Baladan insisted.

For the first time, the gatekeeper looked put out, but off he went again.

More minutes passed, and then he came puffing back. 'He says he's too busy to see you,' he reported.

'Tell him I'll wait,' was Baladan's reply.

So they settled down for the afternoon. Later on, the gatekeeper got out a chess board and lost very quickly to Baladan. He didn't seem to mind. Then the pair of them tried to teach Ruel how to play. When he'd got the hang of it, the boy played the gatekeeper and very nearly won – but Baladan *did* keep whispering things in his ear. The old man let out a big laugh whenever he lost a piece, and seemed to want to apologise when he finally won. After that, he took them on a tour of the stables to see the horses – they were all beautiful creatures, obviously bred to be fast and agile, and the old man was very proud of them.

'They're top class,' Baladan said, 'but they'd never be strong enough to carry a knight in armour.'

'Of course not,' the gatekeeper replied, 'they're for hunting.'

'Where are your war horses, then?' Baladan asked.

The stable boys who were there burst out laughing.

'What on earth would we need those for?' the gatekeeper said.

Baladan offered to help out in the stable, to pass the time, and the gatekeeper left him to it. Mending tack, grooming, mucking out – there didn't seem to be anything Baladan couldn't do. The stable lads were obviously impressed – and grateful for the help. Ruel got stuck in too, and Baladan made sure the boy learned how to do everything properly. There were a lot of horses to see to – every one a hunter – and Baladan and Ruel were still working in the early evening when one of the knights came into the stable where they were. He'd come to get his horse to ride down to his house in the town. Baladan asked why he hadn't sent his squire for the horse, and the knight said he'd lost him some months ago and hadn't found a replacement yet. He introduced himself as Sir Achbor.

You wouldn't usually get a knight talking with a poor-looking man like Baladan, but the two of them chatted easily, as if they were equals; and it struck Ruel again that Baladan must really *be* a knight after all. Certainly Sir Achbor seemed to think that despite Baladan's poor clothes he was talking to a man of his own rank. It was something about the way Baladan stood up straight and relaxed, and looked Sir Achbor in the eye that did it – if it had been any of the villagers, even the proud Maaz, he'd have been bowing his head in front of a knight, muttering his words, and looking at the ground.

The result of the meeting was that when Baladan had explained why he and Ruel were there, Achbor offered to put them up – and the rest of the group – at his house, until Baron Azal could see them. So they told the old gatekeeper to send word to Sir Achbor's when Baron Azal was free, and followed the knight as he walked his magnificent horse down into Kiriath.

'Baron Azal says Baladan's not needed,' Ruel reported to the rest of the twelve.

Zabad and Zilla had rounded them all up, as instructed, and they were eating together in a dark, smoky corner of the Tavern. Baladan had sent Ruel to get them and bring them to Sir Achbor's.

'He says Baladan will have to go somewhere else to look for The Dragon,' Ruel went on.

'Fine,' Chilion commented, 'but if he does, that's no business of ours.'

There were noises of agreement.

'That's right,' said Thassi. 'We followed Baladan to get rid of The Dragon and find the treasure, and that's what we've done. We all saw it fly away.'

'And if it ever comes back,' Chilion continued, 'Azal's the man to see to it. He's obviously got things well sorted here – this place is brilliant.'

'It's great,' said Rizpa. 'I haven't had such a good time in years.'

They'd *all* had a good time that day. They'd been swapping stories about what they'd been up to over supper, and now they started all over again for Ruel's benefit.

He didn't seem impressed though. And when they asked him what he and Baladan had been doing, he couldn't manage to sound enthusiastic, even about the juggler and his fire sticks. But nothing could bring down their high spirits. They all thought it was wonderful that they were going to stay in Kiriath until Baron Azal saw Baladan.

'Let's hope he keeps him waiting a year!' said one of Thassi's friends.

It was only Lexa who saw how upset Ruel was getting. She came and sat by him and asked him what was the matter.

'We're supposed to *kill* The Dragon, not just get rid of it,' he said. 'We have to go after it.'

'Why should we?' Chilion asked. 'As long as it's not here, what's the worry?'

Ruel looked at them all and couldn't believe they'd forgotten.

'But what about Safir?' he asked.

Zilla came to sit with him too, and rested her hand on his for a moment.

'Dearie – I think it might be time to let your sister go now,' she said.

'Face it, Ruel – she's dead,' Zethar added – but he said it quite gently, for him.

'She's *not*!' Ruel snapped, and the tears he suddenly had in his eyes were more frustration and anger than anything else. 'While we were waiting around up at the castle this afternoon, I felt it stronger than I have for weeks. She *is* alive! The Dragon must have some other hideout – it must have taken her there – we have to go after her!'

His voice had risen, and the rest of the Tavern had gone quiet. All the other customers were staring. It looked like time to leave.

chapter ten

Baron Azal wasn't able to see Baladan the next day, or the day after that, or any other day that week. Every morning Sir Achbor sent one of his servants up to the castle, if he wasn't going himself, to ask if the Baron could see Baladan – but each time he got the same answer. Baron Azal must have been a very busy man. Which was surprising – because that wasn't exactly the picture Sir Achbor gave his guests of the Baron of Kiriath.

'Life just seems like a holiday as far as Baron Azal's concerned,' Achbor announced one afternoon. There were six big window alcoves in his banqueting room, three on each side. He was sitting in the middle one overlooking the street, with Baladan next to him. Rizpa and Ruel sat facing them on the other side of the alcove. The room was on the second floor, and Achbor was staring out of the window with a blank face. He was watching the townspeople going about their business in the street below. He spotted the young men from Baladan's party walk past – they were on their way to see a ship come into the castle harbour. Zabad and Lexa were helping Achbor's steward with the household accounts. Zilla was bossing the kitchen maid about. It felt to Sir Achbor as if the whole world was happily occupied except for him. He took a piece of straw from the floor and started tearing it into little pieces, arranging the bits in a pattern on his thigh.

'All he does is sit around and talk, or listen to music, or watch his jesters doing tricks,' he went on.

'Jesters?' Baladan asked. 'He's got more than one?'

'He's got about half a dozen! And that's without the acrobats and conjurors and actors. Some people call it "comedy castle" But it seems like a pretty sick joke to me.'

'How come?' said Rizpa. 'It sounds brilliant.'

'But nothing *ever happens*!' Sir Achbor complained. 'The only action we ever get is when there's a hunt.'

'A lot of people would envy you,' Baladan said.

Ruel looked hard at Baladan. He was starting to suspect that *Baladan* envied Sir Achbor's lifestyle. He certainly seemed happy enough to sit around doing nothing. It was obvious to Ruel that Baron Azal was *never* going to see him – you didn't have to be a genius to work that out from the last few days. So what was the point in staying – unless Baladan *liked* it here. Ruel was desperate to be off after The Dragon – and Safir; and he was beginning to think that if nothing happened soon, he'd have to desert Baladan and set out on his quest alone again.

'Tell me,' Baladan went on, 'what exactly is it that bothers you about things here?'

Sir Achbor looked at him a moment, then looked out of the window again. 'It just feels like a sham,' he said quietly. 'Nothing feels real. *I* don't feel real – I'm not a real knight at all.'

'What do you mean?' Rizpa said. 'You've got a big stone house, and servants and pots of money.'

'That's not what makes a knight,' Sir Achbor told her. 'A true knight should win his knighthood on the field of battle.'

'Where did you win yours then?' Rizpa went on. 'On a fair ground stall?'

Baladan looked at her sharply and she apologised.

'No need to be sorry,' Sir Achbor told her, 'I might as well have done. I was made a knight by Baron Azal when I killed a stag in the hunt. It's the same with all his other knights – the only battle we've ever seen is against dumb animals – it's pathetic.'

He brushed the little bits of straw off his leg, and tapped his foot impatiently.

'Even my squire's put me to shame,' he said. 'He ran away from my service in search of adventure.' Rizpa and Ruel looked at each other, as they both suddenly realised where they'd heard the name Sir Achbor before. They looked at Baladan, but he was giving nothing away – after all, he had sworn the healed squire to secrecy in the forest. Why *was* Baladan so secretive? Ruel asked himself for the hundredth time. It made it so difficult to trust him. Right now, Baladan was looking very hard at the young knight, and Sir Achbor was looking just as hard out of the window.

'And now he'll know something I'll never know,' he said.

'What's that, my friend?' Baladan asked him gently.

'Whether he has any courage,' Sir Achbor replied. 'I wonder if I should be led by my squire and go in search of adventure myself. All the older knights – the *real* knights – did that years ago.'

'No,' said Baladan, and Ruel was surprised by the firm way he said it. 'You must stay here,' he went on. 'There's work for you to do.'

Sir Achbor looked at him as if he was mad. '*What* work?' he asked.

'Wait and see,' Baladan told him.

❧

'Wait and see!' Ruel mimicked, sarcastically, when he told Zilla, next morning, about the conversation. 'That's all Baladan *ever* says. What do you think he's up to, Zilla?'

The pair of them were in the little cobbled courtyard on the other side of the house from the street. Ruel was in the middle of saddling Sir Achbor's horse – showing off the skills he'd learned.

'I don't know, dearie – and I'm telling you the truth,' she said.

'Do you think maybe he's really been working for Baron Azal all along?' Ruel asked her. 'I mean, he *did* see The Dragon off – and Baron Azal's the only one who's supposed to be able to do that. Maybe he's Baron Azal's champion. Maybe he's been leading us to Kiriath all the time just to get us to accept Azal as protector of Hazar. I don't think he cares about Safir at all.'

Zilla didn't reply. She just stroked the horse's mane. It was a beautiful animal – the colour of a chestnut. And its coat shone like a chestnut too, after all the work Ruel had been doing on it recently.

'One thing *does* puzzle me,' she said at last, 'and that's why Azal won't see Baladan now.'

'What do you mean "now"?' Ruel asked.

'Don't you remember?' she said. 'When he was in Hazar, helping build the houses, Azal sent some soldiers to get Baladan to come and see him – and Baladan sent them away with a flea in their ear. Azal wanted to see him *then* right enough, so why won't he see him now he's finally come to Kiriath?'

'When I was in Hazar, Azal didn't know who I *was*,' said a familiar voice. 'Now, he does.'

A flight of stone steps led down the outside of the house from the big hall on the second floor. Baladan was standing at the top of them. Ruel and Zilla had no idea how long he'd been there.

Zilla stared up at him. 'Who *are* you?' she asked, with a sort of nervous tremble in her voice that Ruel had never heard before.

Baladan said nothing for a moment, then smiled. 'About Safir,' he said to Ruel. 'Have you seen the kitchen maid this morning?' and he went back inside the house.

The kitchen was on the ground floor, and had a little door leading into the courtyard. Ruel went hurtling through it in search of the maid.

A moment later he was back in the courtyard, dragging the girl behind him by the wrist.

'Look!' he shouted to Zilla, 'Look at her girdle!'

Straight away Zilla recognised the pale brown cloth round the girl's waist and the little design of flowers. She couldn't have forgotten that that was the material from Safir's dress even if she'd wanted to. Ruel seemed to get out the matching strip that had been on the squire's arm nearly every day. He kept it inside his tunic, and slept with it under his pillow.

'Where did you get it, dearie?' Zilla asked, trying to calm the startled girl.

'I never stole it, honest,' she said. 'If it's yours you can have it. I found it. It was just outside the town gate.'

Ruel let go of the maid and went leaping up the steps two at a time to get to the hall. 'Baladan!' he shouted at full volume, and Zilla could hear her young friend's voice echoing through the house as he ran about inside yelling for their leader.

A few minutes later, he came back down into the courtyard, to find Sir Achbor holding the horse's bridle, and chatting to Zilla.

'Fine trainee squire you are,' he said, 'leaving my horse roaming around, half ready.'

'I can't find Baladan,' Ruel said.

'Baron Azal goes a-hunting today,' Sir Achbor told him, 'and so do I, if you'll finish preparing my horse. Baladan seemed very interested when I told him this morning. Maybe he's gone a-hunting too!'

The horses were lathered with sweat. They'd been riding hard all day – and all day long, groups of servants had been going to and fro, carrying dead animals up to the castle then going back to the forest for more. The main paths were dark with dripped blood. There was going to be a real feast tonight and no mistake. It had been a great day's hunting – lots of wine drunk from the leather flasks tied to the knights' saddles, endless horn-blowing and singing and jokes. Everyone was ready for home now – a wash and a change of clothes, then the party. Baron Azal was just going to give the order to go back when there was a sudden shout.

'My lord!' It was Sir Achbor, and he was pointing away to their left. There, in the shadows of the undergrowth, was a sight to set any huntsman's heart racing – a magnificent boar.

It was half as high as a man, with tusks the size of daggers and tiny eyes that seemed to twinkle with cheek, saying, 'Come and get me – if you can!'

Baron Azal didn't think twice. 'To the boar!' he shouted, and swung his horse round.

The forest exploded into action. The boar was away, crashing through the bushes like a battering ram, and all the huntsmen were stampeding after it shouting and blowing their horns. It was going to be a brilliant end to the day.

They chased it for half an hour. For something so big and clumsy looking, it could move incredibly fast. But then, at last, everything came to halt. They'd run the beast into a dead end made by a sort of horseshoe of craggy rocks. The huntsmen formed up in a line, blocking the open end of the horseshoe, and there was no way out for the boar. It paced around the rocky walls, realised it was trapped, then turned to meet its enemies for the final showdown. Only one man had the right – and the duty – to face a beast like this: it had to be the Baron himself.

They were all shattered from a hard day's riding, but Baron Azal was so excited he vaulted out of his saddle like a gymnast. There was a small area of clear ground inside the horseshoe of rocks, and the boar squared up in it like a boxer in a ring. Even after all that running its little eyes still seemed to be saying, 'Come and get me!' Azal grabbed the spear that hung from his saddle and raised it over his head. He shook it at the boar and gave a roar that echoed round the rocks.

If the boar was magnificent, so was Baron Azal. He had golden, curly hair falling to his shoulders that seemed to light up the shady forest glade; his face was wide and open and honest; he had bright blue eyes that made people smile whenever he looked at them; his back was broad and his chest deep; his legs muscular and strong as tree trunks. He was in his mid-forties but looked half his age. He was everyone's hero, and all his knights cheered at his roar.

But before Azal could make a move another figure stepped into the little arena. No one quite saw where he'd come from, but he must have been hiding somewhere amongst the rocks. The cheering died away into gasps of horror as the stranger strode towards the boar. They could see he carried a sword, but it was sheathed, hanging down his back; his cracked leather clothes would be no protection – if he got any closer, the boar would rip him to bits. But although the man went right up to the beast and stood beside it, the boar never moved. Neither did anyone else.

Then the man reached with both hands over his left shoulder, and in a great swinging arc of light that made the horses rear, he unsheathed his sword. He made no move to attack the boar but stood still and silent facing the hunters, with his sword at the ready. This was obviously some kind of challenge to Baron Azal, and the knights looked towards him to see how he would react. They were shocked to see the confidence drain from his face and body.

His spear point dipped, and it looked as if he'd have made a run for it, if it weren't for all of them watching.

At last Baron Azal made a great effort and broke the spell that seemed to have taken hold of him. 'I told you,' he shouted, 'I don't *need* a dragon slayer!'

'No,' Baladan replied, 'but your people do!'

And with that, he sprang across the space between them. The instant Baladan moved, Sir Achbor was out of his saddle and launching himself forward to defend his lord. But before Achbor could reach them, and even before Azal could raise his spear in some kind of defence, Baladan's broadsword had sliced through the air and caught Azal square in the ribs, nearly cutting him in two.

Sir Achbor came hurtling on towards his traitorous guest, swinging his sword with a wild battle cry. Baladan parried the blow and stepped back. Achbor raised his sword again, but before he could take another swipe at Baladan he heard a sound behind him that was so terrible he checked and turned. It was coming from the dying man, but it was a noise more like a growl than a groan. All of the hunters watched in horror as the body of Baron Azal began to change before their eyes.

It started to swell until the blood-soaked hunting clothes ripped open, revealing green scaly skin. Azal's arms burst his sleeves into tatters and fanned out into great leathery wings that trembled in agony. The men backed their frightened horses away as the thing began to fill the glade. They saw their lord's handsome face on the end of a snaking neck stretch out into a long, green snout from which a thin trail of stinking smoke drifted up into the trees. Lastly his eyes turned yellow as gold and blazed for a long moment with a hatred a hundred times more frightening than the eyes of any boar. Then they closed – and the huge dragon that lay before them was dead.

'It's Hanan. I *know* it's Hanan,' Zilla said excitedly.

'How can you be sure?' Ruel asked her. 'You can't see a thing under all that hair.'

They were both watching something that you could only just be sure was a man, being led away to one of the private chambers in the castle of Kiriath. He was bowed over, dressed in the foulest rags, and his hair and beard were so matted and overgrown that, as Ruel said, you couldn't see anything of his face. On top of that he stank so badly that you could smell him the length of the great hall where they were all gathered. Baladan had led the shocked knights back from the hunt and the first thing he'd done when they got to the castle was to send a search party into the dungeons. This poor creature was what they'd found.

'I just *know* it's him,' said Zilla. 'Who *else* could it be? This is where he was brought all those years ago. Baron Azal must have kept him locked up ever since.'

The great hall was buzzing. All the knights and squires and courtiers were there, and the rest of Baladan's twelve – Sir Achbor had ridden to fetch them whilst the other huntsmen were making their way back to the castle. No one had the slightest idea who the mystery prisoner might be, or how the Baron had turned into a dragon. And they didn't know what to make of Baladan either – was he the killer of their lawful lord who should be torn apart and hung in pieces from the castle walls, or was he a dragon slayer – a hero who'd just stepped out of the story books into real life before their eyes? Even the hunters who'd been there at the kill couldn't quite get it straight, and as for the rest, they were almost hysterical with wild theories.

And they had a long time to wait before they got any

answers – over an hour while a small group of page boys shaved, trimmed, washed and dressed the wretched creature from the dungeons. But when it was done, a fanfare was blown and Baladan led the man back into the great hall. He led him straight to the raised platform where the Baron's golden seat was placed. The fanfare had silenced everyone, and now there were gasps – not just because Baladan was leading the man to the Baron's seat, but because now he was cleaned up and properly dressed they recognised him – or thought they did.

The eyes may have looked dazzled and bewildered, but their bright blue was unmistakable. The face may have been lined and pale but its broad, honest features were ones they knew so well. The white hair should have been golden, but still it fell in familiar curls to his shoulders. And although his body was bent from years chained to a wall, those shoulders were as broad as only one man's had ever been in this hall. On top of all that, he was wearing Baron Azal's finest clothes of cloth-of-gold, and they might have been made for him. They all blinked and stared, and looked at each other speechless, then stared again... Surely... It couldn't be... How was it possible?

Baladan settled the man into the golden seat and turned to the stunned crowd in the hall. 'Allow me to introduce you,' he said. 'This is your rightful lord, Baron Azal of Kiriath.'

The place went wild with jabbering voices, then one rose above them all, shouting out to Baladan, 'But you killed him this afternoon!'

Baladan's voice boomed out loudly, bringing them all back to silence. 'Those who were in the forest this afternoon know what I killed,' he said. 'It was a dragon. It was The Dragon that has terrorised this whole land for a generation. The Dragon that twenty years ago, caught your young lord unawares in the forest, made him a prisoner and stole his shape. The Dragon was a shape-shifter – and as long as it kept the real Baron Azal alive in the dungeons here, it could continue to hide inside his shape. For twenty years it has plundered far and wide and made Kiriath rich on stolen goods. For twenty years Kiriath has been safe from The Dragon because it was the *home* of The Dragon. What better hiding place for a dragon than the body of a man?'

You could almost hear people's brains whirring as they tried to take all this in. Then another voice called out. It was Zabad – The Reaper – The Dragon's servant. He seemed more shocked than anyone to find that the master he thought had lived on a mountain had really been sneaking away to the castle of Kiriath all this time. 'I don't understand,' he said. 'Why should The Dragon have to *hide*? *Nothing* could stop it. He destroyed everyone that ever stood against it. Who on earth was it hiding from?'

'It seems only the dragons know that dragon slayers don't just live in story books,' Baladan told him. 'The Dragon was hiding from me.'

It was then that Ruel noticed something. Looped around this new Baron Azal's belt and hanging just beside his dagger sheath was something like a handkerchief – it was made of pale brown material, decorated with tiny flowers. Straight away, the boy was on his feet and pushing his way through the crush of people.

'Where did you get that!' he shouted, jumping onto the platform.

'Azal wouldn't let us take it from him,' Baladan explained, holding onto the boy as he tried to grab the cloth.

'She told me to keep it,' Baron Azal said. It was the first time he had spoken and his voice was weak and cracked. "Keep it for my brother," she said. They were dragging her past my cell. She hissed the words to me, and dropped it through the bars.'

'She's *here!*' Ruel shouted. '*That's* why I felt she was alive so strongly when we came before. Quick, Baladan – we've got to get her!'

Ruel wanted to lead the search party, but Baladan forbade it. He said the dungeons weren't a fit place for any child to go, and he sent off a squad of soldiers to do the job. It was strange, but no one seemed to question that Baladan was in command – every order he gave was obeyed at once. His next order was for the feast they'd all expected at the end of the hunt to begin straight away.

'You've got more to celebrate than you've ever had in your lives,' he told them all. 'The Dragon's dead, and your lord is back where he belongs!'

And so the party got started and everyone threw themselves into it for all they were worth. Everyone except Ruel, that is. He couldn't eat, and he couldn't sit still whilst the soldiers were away. Zilla and Zabad took it on themselves to look after him, and they had a job to keep him in the hall.

It was towards the end of the first course, when the acrobats were just getting warmed up to give a display, that there was a stir at the main door at the end of the hall. Ruel could see soldiers coming through, and people moving sharply out of their way. They seemed to be carrying something – it was some kind of stretcher. Ruel jumped up and ran to meet them. As he did so, the whole hall fell into horrified silence. Ruel pulled up dead in front of the stretcher and stared at what was lying on it. The silence lengthened, then Ruel threw his head back and howled until the roof echoed. On the stretcher lay a human skeleton.

In an instant, Baladan was by Ruel's side. He was kneeling and holding the boy tight.

'Ruel, Ruel, it's all right,' he said. 'These are *old* bones – they're *Hanan's* bones – look!' and he pointed towards the door.

Ruel looked, and coming through the doorway he saw another soldier with his arm round a staggering figure wearing a ragged brown dress.

'Safir!' he shouted, and launched himself towards her like a shot from a catapult.

The boy cannoned into the poor soldier with such force that he clattered him into a heap on the stone floor, weapons, chain mail and all. The next moment it wasn't a Kiriath guard who was supporting Safir, but her brother Ruel who was bringing her in to the feast.

❦

In the days that followed, Safir was nursed back to health at Sir Achbor's house. Chilion – always keen to be the first with any news – volunteered to make the journey back to Hazar; and soon Naama, Ezer and Maaz were at Sir Achbor's too. Maaz had seemed like a broken man after the retreat from the mountain, and now he sat with tears running down his face as his daughter told him the story of how The Dragon had decided not to eat her but to have her as his wife, so that the false Baron of Kiriath could have a lady by his side. She'd refused point blank and so he'd locked her up and said he'd only let her out when she agreed.

Safir was young and strong and her recovery went well. But Baron Azal had been imprisoned almost half his life, and it was obvious that he was going to be too weak to rule in Kiriath for a long time to come. Rumours of this set off some ugly talk in the town. The whole business in the forest was a mystery to most of the townspeople. All they knew was that they'd had a strong, fit lord who ruled over a land at peace, and now thanks to Baladan they had a weak man in the castle and an uncertain future. Baladan frightened them – there was all kinds of gossip about who he was and what he wanted. Even the knights who had seen what had happened with The Dragon were uneasy. Did this Baladan mean to take over for good in Kiriath? And who was he anyway? – nothing but a woodsman with a big sword.

And so it was that one day when the knights were gathered in the great hall at the castle, they came to a decision. They would go to Sir Achbor's house and have it out with Baladan. They'd thank him for what he'd done but tell him it was time for him to leave. They didn't set off for Achbor's straight away, though. The reason they were all together was that they'd been summoned by Baron Azal, and he hadn't come into the hall yet to tell them what he wanted. They thought it would only be polite to put their plan to Sir Achbor, too, and he wasn't there either. He was in Baron Azal's private chamber.

The pair of them came out together after half an hour, and Baron Azal had Sir Achbor stand beside him on the platform at the end of the hall.

'My noble knights,' Baron Azal began, 'it must be clear to you, as it is clear to me, that I am far too weak to govern Kiriath at present – or maybe ever. This town must have someone to rule it in my place – someone who has proved their courage, and their loyalty— '

This was too much for the knights, and one of them shouted out, 'We'll never have a woodsman lording it over us!'

Baron Azal looked at him in surprise. 'I wasn't thinking of Baladan,' he said. 'When Baladan attacked the man you *thought* was your rightful lord, which one of you came to his defence?' There was silence. 'I've heard the story,' Baron Azal went on, 'and there was only one knight who tried to defend his lord that afternoon. He's standing beside me now. That's the kind of ruler that Kiriath needs – loyal and brave. So it's Achbor that I name to govern in my place.'

Just at the time this was being arranged at the castle, there were some plans being made at Sir Achbor's house as well. Baladan's friends were deciding what they were going to do next. Rizpa and Lexa said they were going to go back home to Maon and let everyone know the good news about The Dragon. Zilla had had long talks with Zabad to try and convince him that he should come home to Hazar. She thought there was a chance his old village might consider accepting him back now – they might even accept *her* back for that matter, she told him. Zethar was going to see if he could enlist in the Kiriath guard and he'd talked Chilion into joining him. Thassi and his friends had an idea they might pay a visit to Maon – there was obviously a shortage of men there, and they were of the age to be looking out for wives. As for Ruel – he just wanted to be wherever Safir was, and anyway he was too young to be doing anything apart from going home with his family – at least that's what his mother said.

This planning session was suddenly interrupted by shouting from the street. As they'd never had any trouble with The Dragon, the townspeople hadn't entered into the spirit of celebration in the same way the villagers had, so it didn't seem likely the noise was to do with revelling. Baladan's friends went to the windows to see what was going on, and they didn't like what they saw. People were gathered in a crowd round the house and were shaking their fists at it. From the looks on their faces, they'd whipped themselves up into a fury and it seemed as if they'd been down to the Tavern first. The shouting formed itself into a chant: 'Baladan! Baladan! Out! Out! Out!' over and over again.

'Where *is* Baladan?' Lexa asked.

The last they'd seen of him, he'd been going down to the little stable in the courtyard to have a look at Hesed, who'd been stabled there all the time they'd been at Achbor's. Maaz went to find him, but he was back in a minute.

'He's not there,' he said. 'And neither's his horse.'

It was Zilla who thought to ask in the kitchen. She came back with the maid.

'He's gone, right enough,' the old woman said, 'but he's left a message with the girl.'

'He says there's more work to do,' the maid told them. 'He says you're to wait here till he sends for you.'

AUThOR'S NOTE

I was sitting at home, relaxing one evening towards the end of the week when the phone rang. It was my old friend Michael Taylor. He was just ringing to let me know he'd be coming to hear me preach at the children's service at our church on Sunday.

'Great, see you there,' I said, and put the phone down. Then I put my head in my hands. I'd forgotten it was a children's service, and I'd been busily preparing a sermon for adults all week! I lay down on the settee, closed my eyes, and asked God to send me a story to tell on Sunday – and be quick about it! He did, and that's how the stories in the Rumours of the King trilogy got started.

The story I told that Sunday morning was inspired by one of the Bible readings for the day, which was from the Gospel of Mark. Afterwards, I wondered if I could take other bits of Mark's Gospel and use them as the inspiration for more stories about the dragon slayer and his friends. So that's what I did, and I soon found there was enough material to make three books! *Out of the Shadows* was inspired by some of the things that happen in the first five and a half chapters of the Gospel of Mark. The other books in the trilogy, *What the Sword Said* and *The Empty Dragon* use material from the rest of Mark's Gospel.

Steve Dixon

If you've enjoyed this book, why not look out for the next title in the Rumours of the King trilogy, *What the Sword Said.*

Turn the page for an extract from the exciting opening of Book Two.

WHAT THE
SWORD
SAID

CHAPTER 1

In his short life Ruel had never seen anything like this weather. Not that he could see much at the moment. The snow was driving into his face so hard that he had to keep his head down as he struggled on through drifts that were almost up to his knees. At 13, he couldn't remember many winters, but Zilla, the oldest of the adults who were with him, could remember more than 50, and she said it was the worst she'd known.

Ruel wondered how his friend Zilla was managing to keep going. He forced his head up and narrowed his eyes as the icy sting of the snowstorm lashed his face. He could just make her out about twenty metres ahead and to the left. Normally her rainbow coloured gown was the thing to recognise her by, but in this weather she was wrapped up in a thick woollen cloak, as they all were. And anyway the dull light turned everything that wasn't white to some shade of grey. It was late afternoon, but the light had been the same since early morning when they'd set out from the mud huts of the village where they'd stayed the night before.

They were travelling in open moor land – nothing to see,

not a rock or a tree or the slightest scrap of shelter – just rumpled blankets of snow on every side, disappearing into grey snow-filled mist. Visibility was poor, and it was vital not to lose sight of each other. Earlier, Zethar – the young hot head who seemed to have taken charge of the group – had tried to get the 12 of them marching in a column; but as the hours passed, exhaustion and disorientation had gradually made them lurch and stagger away from each other, and now they were scattered dangerously far apart.

Ruel let his chin drop to his chest and once again his world became a circle of snow about two metres wide, directly in front of his plodding feet. He couldn't feel his feet. They were way beyond pain – just dead blocks that were carrying him along. His hands were completely numb too, and there were icicles in his hair. They had been travelling through snow like this each day for a week now, and there was no sign of any change. The first day the snow had started to fall it had been like magic – huge flakes the size of butterflies, floating and drifting and turning the world into fairyland. They'd had snowball fights and even Zilla and Zabad had joined in. But that all seemed a hundred years ago now, and Ruel felt as if he'd be glad never to see another snowflake as long as he lived. He wondered how much longer he could carry on: which would break first – the weather, or him?

The other possibility, of course, was that they'd get to the end of their journey. But the worst of all they were going through was that they didn't know when or where their journey *would* end. Their instructions were simply: 'Go to the west of the Old Kingdom as far as you can, and meet me at the castle by the sea.' The problem was that they had no map of the Old Kingdom, and no one in any of the places they stopped could tell them more than the distance to the next village west.

The 'me' who'd given them these strange orders was Baladan, the slayer of The Dragon of Kiriath. Ruel and his friends had helped Baladan in his campaign against The Dragon, but he'd left them soon after the adventure, telling them to wait in Kiriath until he sent for them. They'd waited from summer until the beginning of winter before word arrived. And when it did, they couldn't even be sure the message was *from* Baladan: it had come by word of mouth from a page boy, who'd had it from a travelling beggar, who'd had it from a woodsman, who'd had it from who knew where. But the twelve friends had all been desperate to be doing *something*, so they'd set off in hope. That had been over a month ago, and here they were at the end of the year, still travelling westward as far as they could tell, and with no idea how much further they had to go.

Ruel was starting to go off into a dream – pictures of the town of Kiriath formed in his mind, little scenes from the time they'd spent there. Then there were pictures of his home village of Hazar – the place most of the twelve friends came from – nestled away in the forest, west of Kiriath. He was with his mother and father and his sister and little brother. It was summer and they were walking through the village together. Suddenly his sister grabbed his arm and shook him violently. Then all at once the summer picture disintegrated in a hail of snowflakes, and it wasn't his sister shaking his arm, it was Rizpa. He hauled his face up into the freezing blast, and saw that she was pointing ahead, where he could make out that Zethar and Chilion had stopped and were peering to their left.

Zethar turned towards them and cupped his hands round his mouth to shout. He had a powerful voice, but the swirling snow swallowed most of it and Ruel just caught one word struggling through the icy air.

'Lights!'

Slowly everyone struggled towards Zethar, gathering round him in a huddle.

'Where?' Zabad asked.

'Chilion saw them,' Zethar explained, and pointed off into the gloom.

Evening was coming now, and the greyness around them was on its way towards black. Everyone stared where Zethar was pointing. But no one could see a thing. Even Chilion couldn't see anything anymore.

'You imagined it,' Thassi said, at last.

They went on staring for a while longer without success, then Zethar set off walking again, and the others followed.

They kept together now, and everyone's heads sank again as they trudged on. Only Ruel forced his chin up, and screwed his eyes against the fierce snow that scoured his face, still staring in the direction they'd been looking. It seemed to him that the snow was easing up a bit and the mist was thinning. He desperately wanted to see lights. He *needed* to see lights. He knew they had to find shelter before dark or they'd die. Then suddenly he *did* see them. For a moment he couldn't believe it. Surely it must be *his* imagination playing tricks now. But no, the lights didn't go away, and they didn't move about either – they were definitely there. Ruel tried to call out to the rest, but somehow it didn't work. His mouth moved, and no sound came. He took a huge breath, freezing his lungs and bellowed. What came out was more like a strangled croak, but it was just enough for Rizpa to hear.

'Stop!' she yelled. 'Look!'

Once again everyone dragged their heads up to stare towards the horizon, and now they could all see the twinkling, surprisingly high up and far away to their left, almost like half a dozen stars low down in the dark sky. They let out a ragged cheer and wheeled to the left, striking out for the faintly glimmering hope of shelter. They were all bunched together and Ruel was right in the centre. He didn't look up again. He needed all his strength and will power just to lift one foot after another. It was only the bodies around him that kept him upright and going in the right direction.

He managed to continue like this for about an hour barely awake, and then he stumbled badly, clutching the person in front. Luckily, it was the solid back of Thassi, and he didn't fall, but he was shaken into clear consciousness and he realised that he was staggering over stones. He focussed for a moment and saw that they were on a rising pathway cut into solid rock. He forced himself to look up, and to his astonishment he saw the walls of a huge castle towering above them. Then a strange sound seemed to break around his head. It was like the roar and crash of waves. After that he felt himself tumbling again, tumbling into blackness, and the tumbling didn't stop.

Taken from *What the Sword Said* by Steve Dixon.
Published October 2003.
ISBN 1 85999 672 8

Also look out for the final book in the
RUMOURS OF THE KING TRILOGY,
The Empty Dragon,
published February 2004.
ISBN 1 85999 746 5

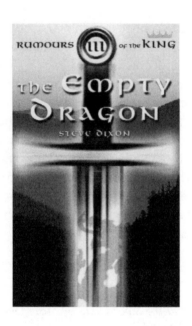

You can buy these books at your local Christian
bookshop, or online at:
www.scriptureunion.org.uk/publishing
or call Mail Order direct
01908 856006